Reasonable
Future of
Humanity

**Reflections about all aspects of human life and the creation
of the state "Earth" with the reasonable coordination**

Reasonable Future of Humanity

Reflections about all aspects of human life and the creation of the state "Earth" with the reasonable coordination

CHOOGIN V. V.

Academician of the Ukrainian Technological Academy,
Professor, Doctor of Science

Worldwide Published by
Pendown Press

PENDOWN PRESS

An ISO 9001 & ISO 14001 Certified Co.,

Regd. Office: 2525/193, 1st Floor, Onkar Nagar-A,

Tri Nagar, Delhi-110035

Ph.: 09350849407, 09312235086

E-mail: info@pendownpress.com

Branch Office: 1A/2A, 20, Hari Sadan, Ansari Road,

Daryaganj, New Delhi-110002

Ph.: 011-45794768

Website: PendownPress.com

First Edition: 2016

ISBN: 978-93-85533-16-7

Layout and Cover Designed by Pendown Graphics Team

Printed and Bound in India by Thomson Press India Ltd.

Contents

Chapter 01

Chapter 02

Chapter 03

Chapter 04

Preface

From all known planets of Solar System only planet EARTH has solid cover with water and air atmosphere with oxygen, which protects from direct space impacts. Ground surface, water and air have relatively small range of temperature fluctuation.

In the twenty first century of a new era all people of the Earth are still interested to know the answer for a question: "What is the origin of life on the Earth?". There are many conflicting theories. However, there is one answer. It is rather simple.

It is known, that a solid cover of the Earth cooled down and after that rock layer with crushed in the form of sand areas appeared on its surface. There is a puzzling question: "Is it possible, that pieces of rock as well as water and gas can invent and create any new living being and plant" or "Is it possible even to suppose, that Mother Nature in the form of stone, sand and air has the ability to consider and thought up by itself all kinds, forms, cover designs of living beings of different purpose on the Earth?". There is one reasonable answer: "No!" It is enough to watch, to feel a stone, sand, clear water and air. Is it really difficult for all of us to imagine the existence of infinite clever living being in the Universe?

Favourable conditions on our planet aroused the Almighty's interest and allowed him to show his infinite creative ability to originate vegetable cover and the whole creation, thinking in the water environment and on the earth.

To start the creation of the live world it was necessary to designate useful circumstances of the Earth living beings life. That is why the Almighty God created conditions for the birth of diverse vegetation in the form of grass, shrubs and trees to perform two functions: protection of the future living beings from excessive exposure to the Sun and their nourishment with foliage, flowers, fruits, twigs. The creation process of vegetation was necessarily accompanied by the development of the aesthetic harmonious image of the whole structure of the plant: trunk, branches, leaves, flowers and fruits. Each plant received nourishment via branched system of the shoots supplied with the special absorption structure of nutrients and moisture. External beauty of all different types of vegetation strikes our imagination by their undeniable, enjoyable, inspiring influence on the consciousness and charm of the soul.

Next to the formation of soil, fertile for vegetation, on Earth's surface, the time has come to the creation of living beings in the aquatic environment of the rivers, seas and oceans. Then the Almighty God has started working out at the infinite quantity of variants of living beings on the land resting upon the harmony of the external cover form and colour proportions, as well as rational functioning of an organism with the reference to specific sources of food and habitat. In this process an extremely important engineering (the modern term) factor of maintenance of effective living beings body resistance to external power influences (pressure force of wind and water) has been used. For example, a tree leaf contains a branched flexible power skeleton of a particular substance. The spacing between the elements of the skeleton is filled by a material for absorption of nutrients from the atmosphere.

The entire surface of the leaf is covered with coloured shell. Surprisingly, the human body is also constructed using the skeleton power with the only difference: the bones of the human skeleton are harder. However, they grow together with all parts of the human body (like the leaves of a tree do).

It is necessary to mention one important point of creation of all life on the Earth. Only Man is given a combination of relatively superior intelligence and the possibility to design, make and use protective clothing, implements, to cook food on fire, to build housing, workshops, industrial enterprises and transport. Other living beings are given other advantages of a person. For example, grasshoppers can jump on very long distances (in comparison with the sizes of their bodies); sharks can gather a high speed of movement under the water surface. And, they use energy of their own bodies, and people on transport (planes, submarines, ETS) is compelled to use energy of oil products or atoms for rather slow movement in space. Besides, sense organs, organs of touch, feelings of surrounding motion, sense of smell, hearing and sight of many living beings are more perfect in comparison with similar human organs.

To preserve living beings' inhabitation on the planet Earth for a long time, the Almighty used two rigid principles: the limitation of all living beings' age, and also the ruthless use of weaker living beings for food. The archaeology testifies to existence of powerful, extensive, significant accidents long time ago. Sharp temperature and air mass structure changes led to the extinction of all big living beings on land, for example, dinosaurs. Taking into account new climatic conditions the Almighty had to start the creation of sufficiently big living beings (including humans) over again.

It is interesting that the organisms of **the majority of living beings on the Earth have the same main components:** a head for placement of eyes, ears, a mouth, a brain for perception of a surrounding situation, a trunk for placement of all main organs for life-sustaining activity, four ÷ six extremities for movement in the form of legs, hands, wings, fins, etc. The principle of feeding an organism with food, its digestion and extraction of useful substances, and defecation is same for all living beings.

Admiration causes a sensation of unlimited variety of beautiful external living beings' shapes. It is enough to recall the Peacock with beautiful shapes and decoration of the head in the form of a bundle with a fan, with the wonderful colour on the spreading wings, etc. Iridisation and shapes, proportions of all elements of the peacock delight all people on the earth. We can observe with a pleasant feeling a variety of beautiful aesthetic images of lions with a mane, giraffes with a long neck, giant elephants, eagles with open big wings during flight, turtles with the powerful armoured casing, chameleons with a dense colourful warty covering and with independent movement of prominent eyes, amphibious legless and having a tail with the infinite variety of beautiful shapes and harmonic colour distribution, inhabitants of the seas and oceans, etc. A special surprise is the variety of lizards appearance, for example, with a raincoat-collar round the head, with a beard from prickly thorns, with a smooth or relief surface. Still the appearance of living beings causes person's delight and excellent feelings in soul and emotion. This fantasy of wildlife couldn't be created by simple evolution of an earth shell. The imagination distribution of a colour ornament of the living being is clearly the highest aesthetic taste of the Almighty's.

As distinct from the infinite variety of shapes of living beings only Man is created by the Almighty in one nature variant irrespective of the individuality of conditions in the different places of residence on the Earth.

Primarily the Almighty put in the mind of the Man the main useful qualities and properties of nature: rationality, fairness, kindness, love for the neighbour and nature, etc. It is good that these valuable people qualities were apparent at all centuries which were known and are still saved. Surprisingly, but in the nature of a person were implemented also the negative qualities opposite to manifestation: hate, anger, selfishness, megalomania, etc. It is difficult to explain the reason of this action. One thought crosses my mind: the conflict of opposites favoured the formation and grounded foundation of good features in Human nature.

Having granted the Man with a high intellectual level the Almighty created favourable conditions for a fast foundation of comfortable living conditions that were carried out on various parts of earth surface. However, disasters of earth shell were threatening. Continental drift, sinking of the developed cities to the ocean floor led to the ruin of mankind civilizations. Once again the Almighty had to repeat the process of mankind regeneration, starting from the minimum living standard. At the same time, God considered negative circumstances of life, behaviour and relationships of all living beings due to the previous experience. As for the Man, the Almighty had to provide for the significant limitation of brain area for thinking. So the modern Man has a considerable seldom-used reserve for the expansion of the outlook where the understanding of the need to live according to reasonable laws of justice and goodwill has been proved.

Nowadays people are aware of mankind development process only for a very small time period (only for 10000 years). The History we know indicates on an unexpected for us demonstration of primitive relations of all people based on cruelty and foolishness. Therefore, the Almighty had over and over again entrusted certain individuals to preach reasonable highly moral principles of life.

It's enough to refresh in one's mind:

- King Hammurabi (18th century BC) who committed "the Code of Laws of Compliance with Life Standards" in an archaic cuneiform on a basalt column;

- The activity of a wise symbol of justice and a perfect leader of Sparta Lycurgus (8th century BC) who established in respect to the Almighty's will brief laws (Rhetra) of equal rights;

- The tolerant dogma of Buddha about the tolerance towards all life beings (6th century BC);

- King of Sparta Cleomenes the exemplary leader of the rational upbringing and education of youth (3rd century BC);

- Jesus Christ the founder of a world religion (1st century AD);

- The Prophet Muhammad the founder of the Muslim religion (7th century AD).

Nostradamus (16th century AD) and Vanga (20th century AD) is an example for many soothsayers of future events in the life of a particular person.

It's notable that, Buddhism, Christianity and Islam preach respect by all human beings on Earth the same basic moral values: the equality of all human beings before God, kindness, politeness, love, caring for others, the usefulness of fair actions, etc.

How does the Almighty gets in touch with a specific person? Very simple! He does not need to overcome a huge distance to meet the person directly and talk to them. He mentally (the same way some gifted people can do) roots his thought in a certain area of the brain. That lucky person may start affecting the Almighty's polite request even not realizing that: "How does it cross my mind?". Certain noble people are allowed to realize clearly their mental ties with the Almighty. If they speak out loud the received advices and instructions from the Almighty's, the people around them with the mind limited with the shades of reality, usually do not believe in that. Such a person is characterized by them as "being insane with delusions of grandeur".

A striking example: young 12-year-old country girl Joan of d'Arc was chosen by the Almighty to fulfil the mission of France liberation. For four years Joan was telling everyone about that noble mission and was declared to be insane by others. Only when she was 16 years old thanks to her efforts Joan was able to start fulfilling the Almighty's request, after her visit to the King of France. So she became a commander and released Orleans during her very first battle. However, after a series of victories in the battles as a result of the betrayal she was isolated from the people. English Court of Christianity found her a heretic and sentenced to death by burning in 1431 AD.

It is sad to state the fact of the moral behaviour of modern mankind degradation (since the XX century) to the lowest limit. Typically, the stratification of society on the basis of people's material well-being of magnitude is accompanied by the divergence of the level of performance of the moral, ethical norms of the human relations. There began to flourish increasingly: the immorality of mutual relations, the audacity of actions and the pleasure by the process of humiliation of others. Accordingly, friendly, good relations of the people are reduced to the limit. As a result, humanity falls into the abyss of chaos! The probability of the beginning of general crisis, repetition of revolutions, wars and mutual annihilation grows today. Well, why to wait quietly, calmly, inactive offensive of the silly beginning of wars on the basis of manifestation of personal benefit of certain megalomaniac oligarchs? Isn't it time to come to our senses? After all, People are the beings endowed with Reason!

It makes no sense in continuing to tolerate this absurdity. Therefore, the Almighty looked for a man with a frank, simple mentality for the obvious thoughts and public presentation of the basic principles of fair, reasonable, the future UNIFORM SOCIETY of PEOPLE of the PLANET EARTH an accessible for ordinary readers attractive form of spoken language: "Question – Thinking – Answer".

In this treatise, to make reading easier, there is RELATIVELY BRIEF description of the reality and the possible paths of all the people in one reasonable, just country "EARTH" for the acquisition of peace of mind, characterized by the concept of "True Happiness". Each part of the treatise is started with the analysis of the actual situation and the statement of facts that nobody can deny. Then there is the consideration of the rational way to solve the existing problems of the original position of reason, justice and benevolence. For descriptive reasons and relief of understanding of the text, all keywords and phrases are highlighted in bold or inclined fonts. This allows the reader to a greater extent emotionally to pay attention to the meaning ("spice") of proposals in accordance with the author's plan. Thus, each simple reader can easily receive accurately designated reference point on creation of the general just state of the Future.

In the treatise the author addresses only to Common Citizens, Workers, NOT to oligarchs, governors of the countries of the world, NOT to scientists, philosophers, lawyers and the other figures, arrogated to itself the right to specify how to and what rules to live by the millions and billions of common people. It is in advance possible to expect negative reaction of oligarchs and bureaucrats to this treatise: indignation of the frank Truth, denial of modern degradation of mankind, sharp protest against offered reasonable, expedient ways of recovery from the crisis and need of creation of a uniform, just, reasonable community of all people on Earth. They will recognise the author as an abnormal person.

There is one hope: in the next 100 years, maybe, there will be at least one reader with high level of mind without "parochialism" modern living conditions and a profession, possessing big activity of nature, power of soul, possibility to broadly inform all people about the good and the evil, the justice and the benevolence.

I wish to a dear reader to play mind and to show energy at the most important responsible point – the moment towards the creation of the uniform beautiful country "Earth".

The author expresses gratitude to the Head of Chair of Branch Translation Theory and Practice, Kherson National Technical University, Radetska S.V. and to the teachers of the Chair for the proficient translation of the book from Russian into English.

–Choogin V. V.

Academician of the Ukrainian Technological Academy, Kherson, UKRAINE

2015

About the Author

REASONABLE FUTURE OF HUMANITY. The treatise is not indifferent for common people to the life in pleasant conditions of justice and benevolence. Common people find it difficult to endure the humiliation by the oligarchs. Thousands of rich people are buying islands, airplanes, ships, and billions of ordinary people have no opportunity to meet even the minimum necessities of life. The result is not a fair situation. Labouring man is living in poverty, and the rich idler sets the merits of his work and lives in luxury. It can't proceed like that any more.

The treatise sets out the common man thinking about the real way to a reasonable, just, uniform country "Earth" on the basis of mutual voluntary unification. The author expresses his hope for demonstration of interest to the treatise by smart people who feel the need and desire to exercise and receive just and friendly attitude for all the workers. Of course, on public awareness of the problem, to discuss ways to achieve the goal and the beginning of the real action will take at least 100 years.

The treatise is designed for all common people to insight into the need of a uniform Earth country creation.

–Choogin V. V.

Acknowledgement

I am very thankful to 'Pendown Press' and its meticulous team who have put their enthusiastic efforts for making this book perfect for meeting my purpose to create an awareness among the common people for living a meaningful life.

Their encouraging teamwork and initiative is praise worthy. They deserve the appreciation as they are participating in a great service of mankind on the earth. Many many thanks to 'Pendown Press' and its team.

–Choogin V. V.

CHAPTER 1

History of the man's way from a Family to a Country and Transformation of Ordinary People Power into Dictator's Domination

No one can refute Human History facts. Many of them amaze our imagination. They are worth to be memorized.

And it puzzles, when the history of certain country is written by a modern narrow-minded expert from his own nationalist point of view. However, people all around the world want to know the Truth of the History, not its interpretation by some individuals.

Creating life on the Earth, the Almighty God endowed a Man with an intelligent and generous nature, which still remains **in our descendants.** But for some reason, with multiplication and development of people relationship, a great degradation of morality, misinterpretation of beautiful and useful man's nature existed during years before and still exists nowadays.

Now God has lost His patience. His hope for Mind endowed by Him in a man, or rather Intellect for providing normal life conditions was not justified. If no clear picture of the way to reasonable future is provided soon, the degradation of moral portrait of Man will continue, because different countries with their subjective leaders will never create rational and fair life for the majority of workers on the Earth.

Almighty God thinks that present day is the right time on the Earth to offer in easily understandable language clear and real program of actions to humanity needed on the way of independent countries, tribes and nations reorganization, into one united, rational country EARTH with its high moral and ethical relationship.

At the beginning of the treatise we will briefly look at the human's life from the ancient time until the present day (XXI century A.D.).

The Way from a Family to a Country

At the dawn of Human's life there were family couples "HE" and "SHE" in the different continents and territories of the Earth. As a rule, parents had 8-12 children. Only 6-10 of them became adults. So, each family increased 3-5 times. On reaching puberty, descendants had a need to create new families. Of course, each family wanted to have its own dwelling and plot of land for procuring food. Firstly, families settled at new territories closely to their parents, but then they were looking for places situated far from their parents' lands. But gradually, relationships between previously unknown people were set more and more often. And because of such a multiplying tide a tribe with the same interest of providing normal life conditions was also emerging. At the meeting all parents of the tribe elected a chief, who was the most active, strongest and cleverest person. He was the man who gave ideas how to make life better.

In a case when something or somebody tried to limit living space of a certain tribe, the chief had proposed the easiest way of solving this problem, which meant to use violence. One tribe armed and robbed other tribes. Then the tribe was gradually subdued and turned into a source of tribute. The problem arose: "Where and to whom should the tribute be paid?" A strong tribe got quickly used to an uneven distribution of wealth, gained without making their effort. From this moment there begins a new historical period of human relationship.

A chief of the tribe gradually increased his share of plunder and tribute. Many responsibilities made the chief acquire assistants. Then military groups consisting of people, who were free from doing agriculture, were formed. So assistants and soldiers began to carry out two special functions: to protect the tribe, and to protect the tribe's chief from the ordinary members of the tribe. The desire for growing rich led to new violence against neighbour tribes, to new wars, conquest of new territories and tribes.

Gradually, family connections in a master-tribe were lost. And a chieftain was delighted with his successful conquests in public more and more often. The chief had an increasing need for implicit assistants. For this purpose, he used a procedure of awarding his guards with fake titles and giving lands or even whole tribes into their possession. All the close idlers obsequiously admired the chieftain. In response to this, they got privileges to violate and rob not only conquered tribes, but also their tribesmen.

All this conditions led to the development of chief's delusion of grandeur. Being strong personalities, chiefs started to believe sincerely in their superiority and unlimited possibilities to conquer more wealth, lands, and tribes.

With the appearance of substantial difference in material goods' possession, tribes began to consist of rich and poor, heads and subordinates. People became pass down this division by inheritance (and not by mental or physical abilities of person). If firstly a chief gave his example and stood in the first ranks of soldiers, then, after expansion of conquests, leaders stayed in their residence safely and sent their subordinates into battle in their place.

The biggest impact on men's consciousness was from preachers of human religious dependence from particular god, such as the Sun, the planets Mars, Jupiter, Aurora, the victory of Nike, the underworld Pluto, the beauty of Venus, etc. With the help of religious figures, the chieftain began to organize his idolization. Then natural need to transfer the power to posterity by inheritance occurred. For this purpose, the procedure of self-idolizing was followed by suggestion to all community of chief's omnipotence, privilege and grandeur of his personality and his posterity. However, for ages not always heirs had the outstanding parental qualities. So degradation of their mental and physical abilities caused the loss of the family power, because the clans of oligarchs and strong figures dethrone "the weakling" at the first opportunity. It led even to changing the direction of tyrant policy, or changing religion (Egypt). Generally, organizational structure of certain community changed gradually from "The Union of Tribes" to "Princedoms", "Khanate", "Kingdom", "Empire".

The human history is an evidence of creating Life Rules in different countries. They existed in form of binding Rules.

We know the names of great statesmen, who have clearly formulated the standards of citizens' life. There were, for example, Pericles in the V century, Caesar and Augustus in I century BC, and Marcus Aurelius, who determined standards of citizens' life in the Roman Empire deeply enough in II century AD. The main regulations of feudal society were established by the Emperor Charlemagne in the Holy Roman Empire in IX century AD.

Since the XVIII century AD in Europe there is a gradual weakening of the absolute royal power and its replacement with the power of the oligarchs and individuals, who have an excessive lust for power. With the development of the industrial goods production in the XIX century, the role of big industrialists increased. The new laws governing the organization and functioning of the governmental authority appeared.

In the capitalist countries, the power was vested to "capital", or rather, to the owners of capital, the capitalists. The ordinary workers were forced to serve as the Executors of the capitalists' will. As a result, the real combination of two meanings – the **Master** (the Capitalist) and the **Servant** (the Working Goods Producer) – dominated.

In today's false "PEOPLE'S" countries Leaders, Presidents, who did not have aristocratic past began to name themselves as "a Servant of the Nation". The formation of "people's" states allowed the oligarchs to relieve themselves cunningly of responsibility for all country matters. The skillfully constituted legislation allowed them to make huge capitals, as if they were made "on behalf of the nation and for its sake."

Practically, people tend to idealize the power of the Statesmen, as if their personal qualities "naturally" match their state position. While the availability of wealth and chief position led to an enticing game of the imagination of an ordinary citizen and the recognition of the Chieftain as the Almighty Person.

Country's Owner

The replacement of the authoritarian tyranny with the collective power of oligarchs (even while remaining only a symbolic power of the king) led to the appearance of various "Empires", "Republics" without great princes, kings, tsars, emirs, shahs, etc. During this period, there was an apparent, false transfer of power to the nation, to the ordinary people.

In today's life, a standard technology of coming to power of energetic power-seeking individuals is distinctly worked out. The power-seeker starts his promotion program with promises. Then oligarchs attract extra funds to the agitation for the needed future Leader, extend his relations, and, practically, ensure his "selection by the nation". At the very first period of his being in power, "the Servant of the Nation" turns himself into the professional leader tending to be newly elected for the next disputative period. This process is tried enough and polished. In such a way, the ordinary working people are pushed aside from the real election process of the people's deputy.

If the country is called as "people's" one, then the real power should belong to the majority of citizens consisted of the ordinary working people, not the rich ones. However, the power formally seems to belong to the people, but the management of all aspects of life remains to be carried out by oligarchs.

The management country system is determined by various Supreme Councils, Governments, etc. Who have to propose rules of citizens' life? The ordinary working citizens or oligarchs' servants? Of course, practically, these rules are constituted and worked out by the oligarchs' servants in the face of "the law experts". Seemingly, everything can be carried out by an ordinary man of the "people's" country. However, in reality, a man has to go through a complicated procedure of collecting a dozen of certificates and identifications in accordance with the laws of the country, government regulations, and local authorities. This comes in the process of "trying to find a white glove in the snow". However, the effective conditions for the enrichment of officials (supposedly, servants of the nation) were created and are created without an objection of supreme power at all times. Alternatively, if there is a "feed" (a payment), the officials of all layers will "stick to the soft posts their teeth and nails" and devotedly serve, praise and support the Leader.

So who is the SERVANT and who is the MASTER in the "people's" country? Orally, all officials of all layers and Leaders serve the nation, work round the clock for the sake of the nation's interests. Thus, the MASTER officially is the nation consisted of the ordinary working citizens, and all officials authorized by the nation are the SERVANTS of the nation. On the basis of these relations, an **ORDINARY MAN, who lives working physically and intellectually in order to satisfy his natural needs without making losses for surrounding people,** and who is not in a public office **has a right to say: "I am a Master, and you** (officials of all layers) **are my Servants!** That is why, we, the ordinary people, (and we are out in millions and milliards), have to determine the formulation, consistency, direction and the main point of all regulations of millions citizens' life." Somehow, none of the ordinary people is able to use THIS officially declared ration of rights in real life.

Therefore, if the country is the People's one in fact, then, of course, all natural resources should belong to the People, and not to the individuals. For example, if lands, rivers, oil, coal, and gas belong to the People, then all income from their usage should belong to the people and effectively and regularly fill the budget of the people's state. Therefore, the current practice of capturing of the legal proprietary right of the country natural resources by individuals is a crime against the People. Moreover, this barbarity slowly and quietly continues to rule in all supposedly "civilized" countries of the planet Earth! As a result, the silent, "quiet" humility with such a barbarian plundering of national resources creates a poor life for the majority of the citizens. Such an unreasonable resignation of all ordinary citizens of countries is a result of the low activity level of Self-esteem.

Unjust Organization of the People's Country Functioning

The management of the country by the leaders of the outnumbered group of citizens united with one idea of their being has the widest distribution. At such an organization called "The Party", the discipline of an obligatory fulfilment of all decisions of the party dominates. The high art of the leader's rhetoric and a delusion of grandeur allow him to promote his ideas and intentions to their performance successfully, allowing him to manage the activities of all party members effectively.

In order to increase the support of their ideas, they promise to all citizens to provide various benefits for assured improving of their life, and they promise to all party members the possibility to function as officials for the fulfilment of the future countries Leader. As a rule, one or several parties as well as representatives of the local citizens' communities win in accordance with their popularity in an election. Then, the

Parliament (The Supreme Court) of the country is formed to pass the Laws, and The Government is formed to implement them.

The party leader gets essential uncomplaining support from ALL party members in the election for the post of the head of the country. After accession to power, the leader replaces the heads of various layers of different parties (or non-party ones) with his pleasing party members. At the same time, their professional knowledge and competence more often are not taken into account, what negatively influences the public affairs management.

If there is a party system of election in the country, the strange situation is created. For example, if 5 parties won in the election. As far as five leaders constantly voiced their ideas of management arrangements in the media, they were those ones for whom the working citizens voted. That is why leaders practically form the composition of the Parliament, for example, they are about 100-400 members. The number of seats in the Parliament for every party is given in proportion to the votes of electors. As a result, only five deputies are really elected to the Parliament. Other members of the Parliament are **appointed** by "the people's deputies" as their leaders. In this situation, "appointed deputies" do not have any moral right to be called as "people's" deputies. Practically, any of the members of the certain party will not dare to vote against the positive decision of the party group (rather, the leader) when passing the law. Thus, the system of public affairs management is created again by individuals and oligarchs. The party leaders' desire and the desire of their appointed deputies to be "professional" politicians of the Parliament has also appeared and rooted.

Negative Rules of People's Behaviour in "Civilized" Country

In the civilized country, the traditional rule of behaviour is observed: after the election, the minority of deputies is **obliged** to execute the decision made by the majority. In the uncivilized countries there always are individuals, who do not want to recognize their defeat, considering their interests above others, therefore they organize immoral actions to failure at any cost an objectionable for them decision. Thereby, they actually show their low intelligence level, an insufficient education, disrespect (or rather, neglect) to the opinion of the majority of the citizens and the absence of communication standards on the whole.

As a rule, False Servants of the Nation possess the high level of admiration of their person, delusion of grandeur and permissiveness. They completely ignore seeing of the vital needs of the ordinary people. For example, they approve, claim and realize the stadium construction for soccer, which costs some billion dollars, and (seemingly) do not have any funds for the supply with clear water and natural gas of domestic needs of 75% of country settlements!

In practice, seemingly, the modern independent professors-experts draft jurisprudence legislations, proceeding from abstract imaginations of professors-philosophers, who are their colleagues. Thus, the majority of laws in all countries demonstrates the result of reflections of people, who are intellectually "blinded" with jurisprudence. In reality, however, in result to narrow-**mindedness** of authors only visible advantage of the law corresponds to the interests of millions ordinary workers. In fact, lawyers pervert a main point, rationality, and justice of the country's laws and protect personal interests of rather small quantity (thousands) of oligarchs. All of this is based on the seemingly "natural, high-moral, due to Almighty" man's behaviour. However, the real equality of citizens' rights does not exist.

The law of the Presumption of Innocence has been used in the civilized countries for more than 2000 years. It is considered as a fair, absolutely correct, and doubtless one. According to this law, only the court can decide whether the person is guilty or not. What is in reality?

In many countries, there is a tradition to violate a woman in any surrounding conditions. For example, periodically, in the cities there are maniacs, who are on the watch at nighttime for women of any age in parks. A criminal hurts a woman, violets and then kills her without any witnesses. If the woman stays alive, then she tells to detectives the criminal's looks when investigating the crime. As a result, there are two persons in the court: a beaten, crippled, and violated victim and a wild maniac. There is an impasse: there were no direct witnesses of the brutal violence, but the court does not have any "legal" right to trust evidences given by only one victim, if there were no any witnesses! So, is it necessary to install a camera, invite two or three potential witnesses, and only then let the criminal violate and kill? However, it is not so difficult to find the criminal having the photo or identikit. Besides, the criminal lives among the people and cannot be completely isolated from them. It is necessary to understand only one simple human justice clearly: it is a crime before the victim and others to hold back and not report to the law machinery about the location of the criminal, because the murderer can kill a few more people, who are innocent! There is only one reason for an immoral concealment of witnesses: they are scared that some worthless individuals of the law machinery cooperate with criminals. This disgrace must be rigidly liquidated in all countries!

Modern lawyers consider that the presence of two or three witnesses for the proof of criminal's fault is obligatory. Otherwise, the court will acquit the murderer! In such a case, the murderer is a "not guilty", popular hero, and the victim, who is the only witness looking for justice in the court, will become a liar and the slanderer! Then the criminal acquires a legal right to accuse the witness of the crime according to the article of the Deliberate Slander with all possible negative consequences, up to a prison! Here is the Presumption of Innocence! One victim as a witness of JUSTICE, does not have any legal right to prove the fact of crime, therefore one swindler, the bandit, as if automatically is innocent. Besides, the violator simply and easily can organize and produce in court false testimonies of false (corrupted) witnesses of quilt of the innocent person! Why the victim is almost deprived of civil rights before "justice"? The court takes the criminal's side and humiliates Truth instead of the fair respect for the Truth. Everything is upside down! Why "legal" laws are made in favour of murderers of the innocent people? Why the criminal has an advantage before the victim according to these silly laws? This is **absurdity! Why the criminal does not have to prove anything and the victim has to?**

There is one more circumstance. The wild murderer can assist the desire to kill dozens of innocent people, but it is forbidden to kill the murderer! The **lawyers** protect him according to jurisprudence laws, according to the silliest interpretation of the rational Principle of Rule of Law! This is with the fact that in practice in most cases lawyers and many other people know for sure that "He" is a murderer. Thus, THE MURDERER HAS MORE RIGHTS according to the justice of the present day, than THE VICTIM, WHO IS THE TRUE WITNESS! The Obvious Nonsense Triumphs!

The repetitive murderer **can** have a wonderful life with impunity at large and in magnificent conditions, or, without any problem, eat, drink, and have free accommodations for the rest of his life in prison. While the ordinary and **innocent people have to** earn and **give their money** to the detriment of their families **for the support of the murderers, prisons and lawyers.**

When arresting any criminal **can be the first, who fires without any hesitation,** but the police officer must shoot in the air at first. Meanwhile, the criminal **immediately fires a shot and can wound,** cripple or kill the law-enforcement officer. Why police officers and any ordinary person have no right without time loss to be the first, who fires a shot at the criminal with a gun, and, in that way, prevent the death of the victim of violation and the police officer! Where is a primitive equity? Ask the ordinary people – "What should be done in such a situation?" The answer for this question is obvious.

Thus, in real life even in the XXI century the unfair supremacy of the legal right of the curtained-off lawyers continues to dominate. Millions of workers and ordinary people – the nation – do not have any right in the constitution and functioning of rational, equitable, and useful laws of being.

The unreasonable distortion of the essence and authority of the human useful high-moral religious also surprises. For example, what for were the confrontations of Christianity and Moslem created? Why did the leaders of Christianity divide a SINGLE trusting in Almighty into different forms of being of the SINGLE religion in different countries (Catholicism, Orthodoxy, Protestantism, etc.)? Any opposition, instead of unity, significantly reduces efficiency of moral upbringing and keeping of high moral qualities of all people.

People, you should think about it!

CHAPTER 2

The Main Things
in Man's Life

In the process of settling (distributing, accommodating) of creations on the planet Earth, the Almighty endowed them with rational qualities, features of their sort, ability to think, make reasonable decisions, and fulfil them.

As a rule, any living being first of all takes care about food, protection from rain, snow, heat and cold. Then, they instinctively care about the necessity to reproduce and create a family. After giving life to their descendants, normal organisms care for food for their helpless kids, and education for them to live independently.

So, let us firstly indicate the main circumstances of Man's life.

Family

The majority of living beings on the Earth reproduce with observing family relations. The Almighty God made everything surprizingly rational. Future mother loses her usual ability to function fully at the period of baby maturation.

She needs a help of another person. Thus, there was a need for the creation on the Earth closest primary community of two individuals "a male and a female" – "a husband and a wife". For example, the representatives of the fauna, the bears, have the following situation: she-bear feeds, grows up, and brings up a bear-cub until he will be two years old. The mother of birds can bring food for her nestlings in her stomach until they can fly and get their food by themselves, ETC.

People have the most difficult situation. A future mother becomes helpless at least for three months. The permanent contact between the mother and her baby after delivery is necessary for the realization of a number of actions such as feeding with breast, taking care of the baby, doing laundry, walking in the open air, etc. It must pass at least two years before baby starts making first steps. The straight father's duty is to take care of his wife and child voluntarily. He has to get food and clothes, help his wife, equip the house with all needed, and protect the family.

The members of the family in order to become closer use the strongest feeling as Love for our Neighbours. Is it possible to imagine that the mother and the father do not admire their child? At first look at his child, the father obtains internal admiration and mood improvement apart from the negative features of his sort. The mother's mind obtains peace more often than father's one does. Besides, in every family, grandparents treat kids with unlimited tolerance and adoration of any desire of their grandchildren. The back child's reaction is appropriate. For any child, mother and father, grandmother and grandfather are symbols of love, a reliable roof and protection from all dangers, and the satisfaction of all her/his needs.

Thus, the normal ordinary people live with the following ideas:

- THE FAMILY IS THE MAIN PRIMARY CELL OF MANKIND,

- NOTHING IS AND CAN BE ABOVE THE REASONABLE OBSERVANCE OF FAMILY INTERESTS!

Health Care + Medicine

Man cannot live fully without health and normal functioning of his body. Getting food is possible only at a normal physical state. Physical and intellectual activities are possible only with the ability to move and think. If there is a pain in the arms, legs, internals, and head, the person is unhappy and is not able to work! The death can come at any age and in any family: family of worker, farmer, king, miner, etc. Therefore, the care of health is the most important circumstance of an intelligent Man's life.

However, until the present day, a surprizing fact remains unsolved: The Most Intelligent living being on the Earth show the most silly and depreciate attitude toward the health of own body! The "Intelligent" humankind neglects the necessary understanding and application of the laws of functioning of muscles, joints, internals, and a brain. Moreover, life will be hard if a body and a soul do not feel calm. Thus, thanks to such individuals as PHYSICIANS, who consciously devote their lives to the deep learning of the natural qualities of a Man in order to help all surrounding people generously.

It is time to realize how necessary it is to be responsible for own life on the Earth, and quietly, peacefully, calmly and continuously to go a light and easy way of maintenance of the health, which the Almighty gave to the Man.

What should we do?

1. In childhood, we must learn the laws of possible body movements, the presence, and function of the main

internals, and the way of an effective development of all that the Mother Nature gave to us! Parents and tutors in day-care centres can and must carry out this function.

From the first year at school, it is useful to continue learning the body and its development; moreover, the practical classes should be conducted in an entertaining form, if possible, in order to make the understanding of rational law of the body movement easier. From the third year at school, it is necessary to start learning the human physiology: the patterns of internals, their purposes and functioning, situations, which are dangerous for the body, the health maintenance procedure, etc. From the seventh year at school, it is obligated to train students for the procedure of the providing of the first medical aid for the suffered person: what is possible and what it is impossible to do in typical situations, how not to be afraid of blood and not to fall in a faint seeing blood, broken bones, etc.

2. In real life the majority of people on the Earth do not consider obligatory to do simple daily exercises in the morning, in the afternoon, and in the evening. As a result, specific hypostases, stagnations, pains in various muscles according to the conditions of the certain activity appear. Strangely and surprizingly enough, but MORNING WORKOUT of all parts of BODY is THE BASIS FOR HAELTH! Especially, in old age, after each rest (sleep) in bed!

It is wise to spend 5÷10 minutes in the morning doing simple exercises. From the beginning, it is very good to set in motion all body stretching it (5 times), make your legs up and down 10 times, and turn around your feet, doing this directly on a bed. Then, it is very good to stand up, turn your arm front and back, turn the trunk left and right, turn the head left and right, sit down 10 times and do one push-up from a position lying on a breast. Such a "minimum" (not considering running) allows you to warm up all your muscles, joints and force sanguimotion in your body.

It is wise to do these exercises one more time in the afternoon and, if possible, add a gentle run along a street, stairs, etc., with the minimum tension in your muscles. In the evening at the convenient time for you, it is very useful for a relaxation of moulded-in strains of muscles and joints to **swim** in a pool, a river, a lake, a sea. It is useful for all people to make aware of this activity, because the Almighty endowed the living beings with the ability to move on land and in water.

It is necessary now to pay attention to the swimming specifics. Only swimming ensures the functioning of ALL without any exception muscles and joints of the living being. Moreover, a tension of muscles occurs in an automatic optimal and minimal mode. A muscle overstrain does not occur.

As a result, **SWIMMING is the most optimal and effective way to maintain the health of your body!**

The question arises logically: "Why there is not any pool in many cities?" Moreover, the majority of cities spent great sums of money on the building of huge stadiums for pleasure of watching seldom performed various competitions and shows. In future after realization of the maximum health effect of swimming it is worthwhile to introduce into human practice of their being the building of small (not for competitions), not expensive, roofed (for both summer and winter) and open summer pools to warm up a body and calm down a soul in any convenience time. It is perfect to have one pool in every block of buildings of the city and in every rural settlement.

3. To keep clean (not to make mass) all dwellings, offices, classrooms, gathering places, and the main thing, which is our body!

4. To provide the systematic supervision of medical personnel for an observance of healthy living conditions for all people, help them to avoid an unfavourable situation, and reducate them. For the fulfilment of this procedure, it is necessary to provide a free access of the medical personnel to people based on an observation of living rules approved by all ordinary citizens.

5. To provide, by all means, a free medical care for all people on the Earth!

   The humankind must live only rational, healthy, wise and effective way.

   It is a barbarity and wildness taking money from a crippled person for a surgery, a treatment course, and a place in the hospital! If you have enough money, your close person, your child, the parents, and the grandparents will live. If you do not have money, they will die in a day, a week, a month...! Moreover, this wild tradition of the present day spreads with rapid rates all over the world in the XXI century! MONEY IS MORE IMPORTANT THAN A PERSON'S LIFE!!

   When will this barbarous phenomenon of moral decadency end of the planet Earth?

6. The perfect way of medical care has been worked out

by the people since ancient times. The family doctor exercises a permanent control of a health and health conditions of all members of the certain family. This way of control provides the foresight of a possible disease of the certain family member, and it becomes possible to take necessary steps, improve physical well-being, and make a man's life journey on the Earth longer. An efficiency of such a medical care reaches the Maximum!

7. Finally to lay open to the public and draw attention of all people on the Earth to the necessity of an understanding of a man's actions on the way of the voluntary destruction of own health! For example, it happens, when doing drugs and drinks, filling lungs with smoke while smoking instead of oxygen, inevitably damaging the body when boxing or fighting ultimately, etc.

   Is it possible to consider a **selling** of kidneys, jaws, nose, eyes, and brain on a boxing ring as a rational action of a person? What about a craving for an achievement of world record lifting burdens, what ensures a soon destruction of a spine? In addition, what about a circus trick on motorbikes with a serious possibility of an accident? ETC.

   WHY do people show such an intellectual "blindness"?

Children as Role Models for Adults

Organizing Human life on the Earth, the Almighty distributed family couples of **the same sample** among all continents and territories of the Earth's surface. Thus, children when communicating with other children and adults do not understand and do not use any piquant concepts such as a colour of skin, nationality, type of the state, etc. They do not care for that, the only thing, which is important, is that a companion in games and life situations is benevolent. Children at once become close and almost dear friends, if the actions of comrades are approving. Children of all animals and even predatory animals (as lions, tigers, etc.) play as friendly and delightfully as they do. Babies unambiguously, certainly, and sincerely know that "a bad one" or "a good one" is their friend. They do not hide such a sincere attitude toward adults of any age, because parents of their peers are just parents loving their children. None of the children ever have a thought to behave in some way taking into account a colour of skin or nationality! They do not want only one to happen; they do not want to suffer from a rough violence, a display of roughness, impudence, cruelty. Normal children do not want to communicate with such "colleagues".

They are those, which **model** of human relationships between all citizens of all countries should be taken by us, by adults!

Unlike children, adults have to use secrecy and masking of their real feelings and opinions toward actions of other people and lie in their daily life! A child, a future citizen of the state, has to grow up in such a negative, complicated situation.

Necessity of Children's Personal Abilities Development

At an initial stage of life on the Earth, it was enough for all people to provide for themselves minimal conditions of their being. Thus, an upbringing of children was limited to the development of their abilities to get food and protect themselves from attack of animals. The progressive expansion of the reflective outlook of people was occurring with the improving of living conditions, the transition from a family area to the community in the form of a tribe, a principality, and a state. As a result, an upbringing of children took new and new ways. An education concerned learning of new, more rational kinds of labour on lands, more comfortable constructions of dwellings, etc.

The division of people's community into poor and rich people, the trade development caused the invention of new ways and means to put down thoughts on a stone, a paper. In the rich tyrannical, authoritative states, there was a considerable need for a use of talented individuals for the progress of the tyrant and oligarchs' actions. This created favourable conditions for the organization of a competent upbringing of children. Found talents were appreciated, encouraged, and awarded, because they brought a maximum benefit for the Leader and the oligarchs.

An urgent task of state bodies in the modern world is also a searching for child's outstanding abilities and a due contribution to development of them. Thus, a learning of rules of high Ethics should not interrupt for any year of school education. Then, an efficiency of talent will have its greatest possible volume.

It is very useful for humankind to peer attentively to children upbringing them at home in the preschool period, or when they play with their friends, etc. All surrounding people have to state and report to parents, if their child has a certain possible talent. A psychologist-physician or an old wise man can carry out the process of the behavioural analysis of the kid most effectively. These actions will allow to provide more effective living conditions for the specific and useful abilities of children to become apparent and develop. Of course, the talent can appear at any age of the person, even in the afternoon of person's life.

What is necessary to be afraid of in the educational process? The people surrounding the Talent can inspire the kid and the teenager with megalomania. This will be a serious omission of an unreasonable education. What should be done in such a situation? There is one easy way out of this: the kid should see other talented individuals. It will not allow to inspire him/herself with "a oneness" of possession the talent, and also "an insistence" on the unshakable worship of him/her and unconditional satisfaction of the momentary desires. For this purpose, tutors have to realize this danger clearly, even if they want to see this student at the top of glory.

There is one more task, which is difficult to be solved: How to keep and not to humiliate self-esteem of children, whose talents have not been detected yet, because, there is a majority of such children! Sensitivity, care, and a sense of proportion are appropriate in such a situation.

The increase in the number of the competent people in different fields of activity always benefited the state and the humanity. A progress of civilization created also a peace of mind in every family of a person acting with success.

In such a rational and aesthetically beautiful way, The Almighty created the main conditions of the progressive being of a Man on the Earth.

Reasonable, rational, natural, useful education for a certain person's life + Moral Upbringing

There is one surprizingly important circumstance: true values of relationships between people HAVE NOT BEEN CHANGED during all known human history, which counts 10 thousand years!

The Almighty endowed every person with love for his or her neighbours. In real life, good human values can be blocked with bad qualities of human nature: rage, wildness, ruthlessness, cruelty, impudence, etc. In this situation, reasonable educational conditions can play an important role! The rationally created conditions of "an up-growing" of the real, worthy citizen provide an operated advantage, a domination of the useful and pleasant manners of people's communication in future human life! As a result, it is logical to say that Upbringing, Education, Development, and Self-improvement are Main Activities of the state educational body in a endowing a nature of a boy or a girl with high moral rules of life on all stages of their life from their birth until the end of the high school.

The duration of the rational and formation period of human abilities for an individual life is practically determined. It varies in different countries: from 13 until 18 years of age. Before a child reaches this age, parents, grandparents, and all family members are involved in the upbringing and preparation for the indication and the realization of the found talents and abilities of their child to live a full and comfortable life.

At the initial stage of life on the Earth, the Almighty created only **working** living beings able for getting food and reproduction. Then, in ancient times, the Humankind created the rational procedure for getting knowledge useful in practice in order to increase the efficiency of labour. Boys and girls separately got a rational education in accordance with the specifics of their activity at a mature age.

After the XIX century AD at school there was a coeducation of boys and girls according to one curriculum. There were frankly negative consequences of this action: the withdrawal of subjects useful for females from the curriculum and **unreasonable waste of time of students for deep learning about those things, which will never be useful in their life. However, the TIME of life is given once to every person, and it will not be returned.** Time is a precious gift of the nature; therefore, it must be spent on the Earth consciously, usefully, and effectively. Because no one knows how many hours, days, years of life the fortune gave, and how much time remains to live! So, why is there such neglect to a reasonable basis of life? How is it possible not to take into account the mission of boys and girls, young women and men?

It is rational to use ONE educational principle: to learn all universal human values in common with boys and girls, and subjects, taking into account specifics of males and females, separately. It is reasonable to distinguish two levels of literacy: "the Obligatory Minimum of Knowledge" and "the Competence of the Expert".

In the first four years of an educational process, it is useful to provide for all children the concept of the variety of all main spheres of adult's life. This acquaintance will allow finding, deciphering natural disposition of the student to interesting subjects, which are pleasant to his/her nature, and unambiguously defining an imperceptions and intolerance of the nature to something. Certainly, for normal life on the Earth ALL people need to be able to read and write, manage arithmetic, know the peculiarities of hygiene of a body, cook, have an idea about the laws of the nature and high ethics of people's communication, etc.

The usefulness **of education** will be maximized when performing one condition: each direction of knowledge has to correspond to individual natural abilities of the student. It is time to think about the way of solving the problem of an individualization of education. This perfect transition is possible in the future of Humankind after the foundation of the reasonable management by all spheres of life in the mini-states.

Why do all people waste their life time at modern school for studying deeply (not for acquainting) some specific specialities? Only some people of million graduates go to work as a physicist, a chemist, a mathematician, a nuclear scientist after the graduation from high school,. How many citizens will use in life the knowledge of the law of flight of a bullet from a gun? Moreover, who from graduates (especially girls, women) uses "logarithms" in practice at least once in life? Etc. As a result, in most cases there is a waste of time, energy and work of teachers.

The truth of life testifies: in practice, children and teenagers are normally educated at school only within the first seven years (1÷7 classes). Further (8÷10 classes) they go to school with a big unwillingness, "at the point of a gun". Short-sighted parents recommend to their young men and girls to get higher education without fail after the graduation from the school. Nevertheless, why is it necessary to interfere with a natural way of life of the majority of girls and postpone the process of creation of a family, a birth of children? In addition, many young men like a profession of a MANUFACTURER, for example: a builder, a mechanic, a smith, a car mechanic, etc. They have nothing but dream about a full life.

Chronicle of the Preschool upbringing and of the Child's Education

The modern equipment of informing allows expanding and speeding up the process of worthy level of education of a Man. However, in reality, the period of the reasonable, rational improvement of the process of the children's education can be carried out not less than in two, three generations of people in 50, 100 years of life of Humankind or more.

First Two Years of Life

The baby was born. The nature endowed it with initial physical and mental abilities.

At the initial stage of reasonable education of children it is necessary to show sensitivity, care and a sense of proportion from the tutors' side, because it is always necessary to solve a difficult problem: "The way how to keep, not humiliate a self-respect of children, who do not have their talented abilities found yet? ". Such children are in the majority.

Parents have to contribute to the development of natural useful for life abilities, the protection from showing the defects of children's nature, the elimination of their physical defects. The role of mother and the grandmother is the most significant during this period.

What is Necessary for the Child?

Certainly, it is useful to receive a good nutrition and nursing, sanitation, and develop mobility of hands, feet, a head and a body. It is useful for parents to carry out education of children using conversations, toys, gesticulation, an expression of emotions, a play of lips and tongue, an admiration of the surrounding world, a quiet music with smooth sounding a natural rhythm (not "wild rhythms of a modern music"). It is also appropriate for parents to find out what the baby likes, what makes its mood better and irritates it.

In childhood, the child learns how to speak and get to know new words for the designation of actions necessary for him/her: "I want to eat", "I want to pee-pee", "Give me this", "Come to me", etc. None has ever thought to teach a child of a language "grammar". Only after mastering a vocabulary minimum necessary for life it is possible to begin the process of knowledge of more correct pronunciation of words considering certain situation.

As a result, the child develops a sufficient understanding of an informal conversation in language of parents for the first two years. During this period of life, a speed and a depth, a quality and a reliability of impressing in memory of new words, expressions are maximal! At this very stage of the child's life, it is useful, expedient without violence, and effective for parents to use these features of the child's nature.

Education at the Age of 3÷4

From the age of three, it is necessary to pay considerably on time attention to the physical development of the child: to develop mobility of joints and the correct movements of hands, feet, trunk when walking, running, jumping, etc. The special attention should be paid to the perfect means of physical development of the child – swimming. At swimming, all muscles perfectly and naturally strain as needed, and all vertebrae in a backbone perfectly settle down and strengthen in a trunk. What is happening when breathing? The better natural intense development of the lungs does not exist.

All children like to dance, take part in running, jumping, and fighting competitions, etc. Therefore, there is no need for violence on the development of their physical qualities. The child plays with delight of the soul, willingly and, therefore effectively! In such a way, a man on the third and fourth years of life lays the foundation for the highly effective future "adult" life in rational option of actions without even realizing this.

From the age of three, the child is able quickly in only six months to master a spoken language of his/her contemporaries and coevals of other nationality only because of a daily natural communication with them, without violence over own qualities, an intervention of adults, and any lessons!

It is useful and necessary for all parents to use this unique circumstance. Following the effective law of the nature, during this period it is useful, reliable "to put down" into child's brain the knowledge of spoken "foreign" language with its correct and native pronunciation. Because studying at school and higher educational institution at mature age, it is impossible to achieve this quality of knowledge of a foreign language without living in the foreign country for some time. For that, it is expedient to organize a direct communication of children and adults from different countries on topics of any simple real life situations on television.

During the next years of life, it is easy for the person to renew the knowledge of pronunciation peculiarities of another language and carry out a free communication with the foreign colleague without irritating them with indistinct speech. During all life, in a man's brain words "thank you" will be repeatedly addressed to parents and tutors, thus, electromagnetic waves will surely bring sincere pleasure to all, who created the conditions for getting knowledge of one more or two languages of adults' communication. After mastering a spoken language, it is possible to start learning alphabetic symbols for the written designation of a concrete sound: "a Sound – a Letter, a Letter – a Sound".

Since ancient times, the symbolic image of words, concepts was carried out by their fixation on a stone, clay tiles and other subjects. Then because of creation of Geniuses symbols-equivalents of a concrete sound in the form of letters, which could be represented by writing on any subject, were born. The invention of paper solved a problem of simple, fast, easy fixation of thoughts of people.

It is sorrowful to establish the sad fact: in real life even in the most civilized countries of the world, for example, Europe, the first developers of writing distorted a formula 1/1 for an unclear reason. For example, they quite often designated one sound with two, three or four letters, and at the end of words, they inserted symbolical soundless letters. Besides, in different words they displayed **one sound** with **various letters** or a combination of several letters. Such an intellectual helplessness (limitation) is not clear, when considering this from a position of a common sense of the normal person (not a "philologist"). Moreover, is it necessary to waste time on writing of unpronounceable letters? Why is it necessary to display in writing and pronounce **distortions of a certain sound** according to a national habit of uneducated people? These distortions significantly complicate an understanding and learning of another language. It is enough for philologists to use the specific designations only in their scientific works. Moreover, it is not necessary to hamper all people to live in normal conditions of communication!

From a position of a common sense, the formula of a pronunciation has to have one rational appearance for its practical use: "ONE specific, certain, and unambiguous SOUND is displayed with ONE LETTER", i.e. "**One letter has to have one sound equivalent**". Moreover, what about the confusing and illogical "peculiarities" of grammar of professional philologists, which are difficult to use? Are they necessary in an everyday life of a simple person? Well, who from adults firstly recollects the name of the necessary case, etc., and only then speaks "correctly"? **It is time to distinguish and use significantly in an everyday life two types of grammars: one for professionals, their scientific works for acquisition of an academic status and one for ordinary people in the conditions of their life.**

Due to the development of international relations, there is an objective process of coordination of high rules of life. Therefore, the tendency of a communication in ONE language naturally formed. It is useful to develop an international language of communication based on equivalence of a sound and a letter for a simple and easy rational pronunciation of the written text. It is useful to use Latin letters with an insignificant addition of letters from other languages as a basis.

Upbringing and Education of the Child at the Age of 5÷6

Being guided by the natural desire, all mothers protect their children from the difficulties of life. As a result, they instil in their children helplessness, weakness. Because of this, in further life, the trauma of a soul and a body of the person will surely occur! The child will be endowed with Weakness and Helplessness, Prostration and Loss of interest for further life, instead of Strength and Firmness! Well, why should we do this thoughtlessness? Please, parents, remember a rigid upbringing of Spartans adjusted for the present day of life.

The child visually shows the tendencies to different types of actions. For example, the child likes to move, travel, ask and argue, to express the frank attitude towards people, animals and their acts, to notice the beauty of wonderful forms of the nature, things, words, and expressions.

At this age, it is necessary to accustom the child to demanding system and working procedure of the future education at school. It is a very difficult task. **All natures are different**, but the system of school education is **common** to all children, for boys and girls, as if they carry out the same functions in life and have the same interests and requirements. Where is such THOUGHTLESSNESS from? This is an obvious crime before future "adult" human life.

What do Parents have to do?

1. To realize, define the existence of a child's limit of voluntary understanding of all new, because at school the child will quite often force himself and work according to the order of adult teachers.

2. To the good of the concept "a Well-mannered Person", it is necessary to designate in consciousness of the child the full program of actions for the

natural, automatic manifestation of external beautiful manners of behaviour (politeness, goodwill, and rationality), anticipation of the consequences of the actions in different situations and prevention from unreasonable acts, etc.

3. It is useful to accustom the child to the observance of behavioural rules, sitting at a table when eating.

4. To accustom the child to rules of patronage upon kids (a sister, a brother, children of familiar parents). This procedure brings up manifestation of care, kindness in the older child and creates the maximum effect of easy instilling of beautiful qualities, which are worth the Man (not the Caveman). Besides, at the development of the procedure of patronage the child understands what the "maturity" means for the first time. Moreover, it essentially, significantly defuses its tensions, internal opposition, and unwillingness to implement recommendations of adults. As a result, there is a high effect of upbringing and the formation of the beautiful and reasonable speed up!

5. To teach singing, because singing by itself is a special, pleasant, inspiring type of behaviour, what raises the person over the earth! Singing develops high feelings and allows seizing an accurate correction of intonation that is very important for a cultural pronunciation of words, especially foreign ones.

6. To teach drawing in the various ways, because drawing productively develops the highest qualities of the person: an ability to imagine the next image of all conceived and represents it on this subject, a piece of paper, a canvas.

7. It is useful for the future life to train the child in versification rules, because the composition of verses

allows to develop imagination, comprehension, selection of words, the management of the smooth combinations of words. As a result, the game of mind of the child, and oratory elements are formed.

8. It is useful to make the child take part in physical and intellectual COMPETITIONS. They significantly increase the incentives of improvement, which allow to improve a possession of the body, to teach to make something, to draw and read verses in front of an audience.

Such a process of education and training creates the conditions for an accurate understanding of the opportunities in the present day of life. In such a natural and automatic way, the process of SELF-IMPROVEMENT of the child will be easily carried out!

At this period of human life, there is a putting down of the BASE of future useful qualities and the measures of providing a peace of mind of the adult person. Therefore, the main duty of parents is a continuous introduction of **the main universal values** in a consciousness of the child:

1. "NOT yours – DO NOT take!", "Do not touch, DO NOT take what DOES NOT belong to you and is a property of another person", "Do not think at all of the assignment and the capturing of anything, which is located in any territory (public or private) in any condition (good or bad)". IT will help you not to worry about your own property.

2. If you see money on the road, just think carefully, politely, respectably – "Maybe, it was a poor old woman or a child, a student, or a pensioner, who lost them? They probably will return and look for them". This is a conclusion: put THEM nearby on a

foreground that people or cars do not trample them.

3. The KIND wish is always pleasant to all of the people on the Earth without an exception, and the manifestation of rage always spoils own mood, health also.

4. BENEFIT people. Before doing or making something think: "Are my actions harmful for other people?"

5. Here is a useful chain of actions:

Intention – Considering – the benevolent Decision – the rational Action- the Analysis of the past – the Conclusion for the future.

As a result, it is possible to state a truth: the volume of work made by parents fully upbringing one, two and more children is HUGE! Therefore, it is not necessary to force the woman to obligatory waste their time on earning money on living. This is men's duty.

School Education and Upbringing

It is rational to distinguish four types of the school education:

"Elementary school"   – **ES**, 1÷4 forms, 7÷11 years

"Secondary school"   – **SS**, 5÷7 forms, 12÷14 years

"School of extensive training" – **SET**, 8÷10 forms, 15÷17 years

"School of vocational training"– **SVT**, 1÷ 2 forms, 15÷16 years

As a result, the student can get an education at schools of different level:

1. "Elementary level of education"– at **ES**, at the age of 11,

2. "Second level of education"– at **SS**, at the age of 14,

3. "Extensive level of education"– at **SET**, at the age of 17,

4. "Advanced level of education"– at **SVT**, in 15 or 16 years.

Elementary School

At the initial stage of school education, it is useful to realize clearly the essence of the concept "the Minimum Literacy Grade" for a normal further life of a Person.

In the XIX century AD, in the European countries spiritual figures reasonably organized Free Church schools with the four-year program of elementary education, which was accurately thought over. After graduating from the elementary school, teenagers (at the age of 11) could count, write and know the basic rules of life. On this base, it was possible for them to start learning a simple craft for making money for their living.

Presently during training at the elementary school ES (at the age of 7÷11), it is also necessary to lay down the same elementary Literacy of all people for the reliable supporting of their personal needs in their future life.

Secondary School

From the fifth form, it is useful to learn universal human values on a full scale. At the first grade level, it is necessary to receive information about the history of human development and that is necessary for life of the adult. Then, it is useful to start the process of learning reading and the writing in native and other (their) languages. It is useful to start to do mental arithmetic (without using the calculator), to learn an alphabet of geography (a location of countries, cities, surprising objects of the globe), and names and affairs of Geniuses of Humankind in various fields of art (painting, music, architecture, equipment, etc.).

In the seventh form, it is useful for a strong sticking to

their memory of the basic rules of grammar **to write letters** for schoolmates under colour of birthday greetings, participation in competitions, travelling, etc. at least once a week. Such a mutual action is a free lesson of the imagination and the training of the students' thoughts formulation without any violence and fear that their teacher checks their literacy level. Besides, it is useful to revive the custom of keeping a personal Diary for the written fixation of thoughts. This procedure is a progress of reflections, mind games, and the birth of new ways to solve the earlier tasks. In such a way the ability to deep reflection on a way to Truth develops.

As an example of statements of the thoughts, it is rational to use classical literary works. As a rule, thoughts of known ingenious writers are represented in the description of historical facts. It is very interesting, informative, and appealing. Over time the especially clearly stated thoughts turn into classical sayings. They are easy to understand and remember. Then, at the right time, people freely and easily can use them in conversation with other people of any age, intelligence, and education.

Everybody knows how difficult it is in practice to learn to express your own thoughts on paper and to write in a logical, smart and good way. Reading the classics promotes training of the ability to think and express your thoughts orally and in writing form, that's why it is one of the most effective tools for a self-development. The level of education, breeding, and intelligence are naturally demonstrated in conversations with peers and adults. Growing of authority leads to a recognition of Intelligence. On this basis high school graduate can be offered to a perspective position with a good salary.

The aesthetics of movements gains in importance in contact of young men and girls during the period of physiological maturation. Look at their moves when they are walking, running, etc. Someone steps with difficulty, puts the feet incorrectly on the ground and does not transfer the feet with step length. They run straining many muscles, when it is necessary to strain only the proper muscles in a rational sequence. There are very few people who keep their body straightly during walking and don't bend forward, while the majority rocked himself backwards and forwards during walking. Do not slouch, it is enough to deploy shoulders and squeeze shoulder-blades. The head should be kept straight (not up and not down). Do not brandish your hands and do not spread them apart in elbows. The form of movements could tell easily whether or not you are well-mannered. It is possible easily and quickly to fixed, rational, beautiful and graceful movements of all parts of a body in a comparatively small age.

The objective reality of being requires taking into account the sexual essence of girls and boys, their purpose in life.

Boy, Young man. Is it possible that future man, father of family, can't, for example, hammer nails or handle wood, metal, work with file, knife, axe, or can't sharpen the tool, safely kindle the fire, connect hoses, disassemble and assemble simple electric appliances (switches, wiring, etc.), measure voltage in electric network, know safety rules. Everything is important to know and to do for a normal household life! This will help not to waste a time in future for calling and waiting for a specialist, especially if you live in village, etc.

Girl, Young Girl. It is necessary and sincerely pleasant for each girl, and then a young lady, to learn how to cook tasty meals, how to wash, iron, cut and sew, dream about her own Image of Beauty and Grace, correct physical development and body changes (nobody is perfect), sing, dance, laugh nicely, etc.

The significant effect in creating high Human qualities is achieved by direct contact of a child, a pupil, and a musical instrument! Therefore it is necessary to have Music Classes in every school, with all kinds of main classical musical instruments for orientation of each pupil spiritual nature.

Manners of Decent Behaviour

Upbringing of refined taste for beautiful clothes and manners is a necessary condition for pleasant communication with other people.

Every person from the very early age needs to know how to sit at the table without spreading elbows wide, how to use cutlery rationally, to eat food correctly with a spoon and fork and to chew with closed mouth, to pour out tea, coffee, wine, etc. But we may say with pleasure about one rarely occurring useful life fact: Procedure of decent taking meal had been already regulated immaculately, ideally without the slightest inaccuracies. This fact can be an example for other actions.

Boy, Young man.. It is necessary to learn a boy since the childhood about simple useful and beautiful procedure of care of a girl and a young girl, and to help girls in any circumstances. Lady may not necessarily say "Thank you" for a natural act of a Gentleman. For example, Gentleman should always be below walking upstairs and downstairs to protect Lady from a possible falling. And how to open the door? There is no definite answer because doors have various designs: lightweight and heavy, narrow and wide, opening inwards and outwards. Lady also can be thin, stoutish or with a child. Therefore it is unwise to stay always in aisle and thereby hinder her to pass. It is better to estimate quickly unfamiliar situation and make rational decision.

For example, the boy/the young man opens a door inside, and the first person (not Lady) enters inside, thereby giving a way and then holds a door until the girl, the young girl or Lady won't pass in the house.

It is pleasant to see and feel high and easy art of gallant or business conversation, to meet gracefully a Lady, an Old man, a respected person, etc.

It is useful at school to organize and take a time for CHARITABLE PATRONAGE of pupils and people! There will be always a lot of people for this purpose. For example, a circle of those in needs and absolutely helpless people, who live in the area near the school, can be defined and given for constant care to pupils. The procedure of patronage will surely bring pupils sincere pleasure, but also upbringing of Benevolence, Respect for people, Decency, etc. These years of studying at school will be certainly remembered at special moments of adult life and will protect from barbarous action committing!

Art of Eating Food

For some strange reasons an ability to cook food in all modern countries is not compulsory for children and teenagers. However, is it possible in this case to consider a Person at least elementary educated? Modern school graduates do not know the properties of each available product, so very often they use it in wrong and rather harmful way for their own health.

Is it really necessary to explain this simple truth that all people, without exception, need to know various products properties for its competent and health usage in everyday life? Individual characteristics and personal needs require eating some concrete products, but we all eat almost the same available food: bread, butter, meat, available vegetables, tea, alcoholic drinks, etc. That is why situations of organism self-destruction by food are not rare. TO KNOW the properties of a concrete product and ABILITY to cook food in a right way with saving all its useful qualities are EXTREMELY NECESSARY for keeping (and increasing) the level of persons health. Relying upon the real necessity of each Person health maintenance, it is necessary to introduce **an obligatory course "The Art of useful and tasty food"** at schools.

Concept of Medicine

It is wonder, but for some reason people all around the world do not want to answer the simple question: "What is the most important for a Person?" Is it KNOWING OF FORMULAS of physics and chemistry, used in life only by experts, or minimum required MEDICINE KNOWLEDGE? Medicine is necessary to ALL people on the Earth. But school knowledge about functioning of all parts of a body and organs isn't given properly in volume really needed for life. Nobody with primary or secondary education will be able to provide competently first aid to injured person, especially during a walk outdoors. Is this 'education' called Civilized? Because of ignorance, in real life all people on the earth accumulate negative consequences of their neglect and lack of care of their physical condition. And as a result there is a shame for bad state of health.

So how can we learn and get the basics of primary medicine in a logical way?

1. At first, you should clearly and without fainting, naturally, simply, visually, slowly see, learn and memorize a skeleton structure as a whole, skull structure and appointment of muscles.

2. Then, you should learn the laws of functioning of the life supporting organs and the brain; also learn elementary rules of preventing unreasonable physical actions and behaviour.

3. Competent development of organism is also achieved by getting detailed answers on a number of questions. "How do muscles attach to the bones? How to develop muscles effectively? Where are the most painful places? How can the injuries occur? Till what age joints restore quickly after the load and when does this process stop working with all its negative consequences? How to help get locked hinge joints mobile again and to prevent their degradation and loss of body mobility?"

4. It is important to remember a few simple obvious rules:

   ➤ do not carry anything heavy for a long time without alternation with rest because the squeezing of soft tissue from joints occurs, preventing the metabolism and rapid restoration of tissue;

   ➤ do not fill the lungs with a smoke;

   ➤ do not use drugs;

   ➤ do not sell your own health in some kinds of "sport" (boxing, wrestling or ultimate fighting, etc);

   ➤ do not injure other person (boxing, ultimate fighting, etc);

   ➤ to be able to give first aid to injured person (for example, to stop bleeding without bandage); etc.

Physical Development

Up to 14 years Nature lays the Foundation of a healthy organism. The progressive formation of physical indicators of person occurs, such as: lengths of bones and volume of muscles, etc. It is therefore necessary to carry out physical training of all children and adolescents, especially those with physical disabilities. At this age it is useful to examine different types of sports for choosing one the most appropriate for individual, and for removing physical disabilities.

At schools it is useful to do warming-up of muscles and joints between lessons every day. For this purpose it is useful to increase the duration of breaks. It is reasonable to equip all schools with pools with a length of 13 m and two showers for carrying out the most ideal type of physical exercises. Swimming guaranteed relieves tension of muscles and brain after all lessons. **A pupil will go home fresh and relieved of strain!** It is useful to visit the sports sections two-three times a week.

Of course, objectively there is a distinction of a physical state of girls and young girls in comparison with boys and young men. It increases with years. Boys have opportunities to protect themselves physically. However, the girls have their own psychological advantage: nobody expects from them significant physical resistance! This "unexpectedness" allows them to place the hands and the body effectively in regard to the opponent in readiness to carry out the appropriate sleight of defense.

The truth of life forces people to anticipate hazards. Therefore protection of girls and young girls against attack of a savage is an indispenzable moral duty of each boy and a young man.

Up to 14 years a volume of muscles is formed. Therefore it is necessary to make exercises effectively and rationally for achievement of two goals: increasing strength of muscles and development of automatism of actions at self-defense. Life practice shows that after development of fast reaction, hands, legs, body move automatically, without thinking, and even before you started to be afraid, feel frightened or «petrify». In this case, worthy rebuff will be given to attacker. It is very important to memorize a typical negative situation: **only** knowledge of self-defence without bringing them to automatic execution will lead in most cases to defeat in battle. This is the reality of life. Years of trainings at least 3 times a week are required for acquisition of automatic reaction. If you've been training for 5÷10 years, automatic reaction becomes a reflex and will work usefully even in old age!

In modern real life different types of martial arts with trendy Japanese names are widely adopted. And lack of understanding by parents of deadlock, useless physical exercises of their children at any age is surprising. For example, the hooligan is very tall and has a large body mass. Will this trasher really feel a punch of a small fist? Your defeat and injuries are imminent in fight with a big opponent. So why should you waste a time and efforts for practicing power punch? The punch at protection against attacker should be not "power", but "right" in the right direction on a weak place of person of any weight and strength. Every person has enough weaknesses: foot, front part of leg, knee, groin, etc. Is it really reasonable to expose your health to DESTRUCTION on boxing trainings? And such OBVIOUS thing, for some reason, isn't noticed by people in all countries! The advertising of ultimate fighting and procedure of sale of (integrity of) a brain, kidneys, heart during boxing programs go on TV screen constantly. As a result, middle-aged fighters of ultimate fighting and boxers leave sport to be in poor health, instead of full living for the rest of their life! Even wealth cannot bring happiness in life. STUPIDITY and UNCONTROLLABILITY again triumph over person's life!

It is very wise, rationally and helpful to recommend pupils going in for sports where they will learn how to impacts simply and rationally on opponent's weaknesses to disorientate attacker. This art excludes receiving of return blow.

Search of Vocational Guidance

Time to think about the future life comes at age 14.

After seventh form the majority of graduates of secondary school are essentially tired of intensive education. They want to have more independence and opportunity to earn money as soon as possible for freer, more independent and self-sustaining way of life!

So it is necessary for any country to have good-organized system of vocational schools provided with the most modern equipment to support this natural desire of youth. Thereby a graduate of such vocational school receives a guarantee of employment or organization of his own business.

What to do and how to earn for a living? To answer this topical question you should try as many spheres of activities acceptable for your soul and body as just possible (do not be lazy!). It is also helpful to discuss this problem with somebody whom you respect and with parents. People with life experience will tell you about their mistakes and successes and said what caused it. Fixing in mind other people life experience will surely help you to avoid unwise and dangerous actions in unclear and unexpected situations! It is also useful not to be lazy trying yourself in some areas of MANUFACTURE of products working with hands and mind. What if it is something that will come in handy!!

Where to approve yourself? At school you can try only few life activities. So it is necessary for you to take the initiative and try yourself at every opportunity. For example, you can help unknown man, woman, neighbors, acquaintances and relatives voluntarily with any activity and to provide disinterested help to old people, people with disabilities, mothers with many children and people in extreme situations. And one important function is carried out during this process of helping the needy people; namely, that pupil does something by himself. So the situation of vocational guidance arises. Girls have their own vision, boys – theirs. They involuntarily think about this and assess measure of rationality, usefulness and reasonableness of some actions, draw useful conclusions and "take good note", i.e. fix in memory the results of mind games and actions.

Results of Secondary Education and Upbringing

After graduating from high school 14years-old teenager should know and be able:

- To know the Latin alphabet and alphabet of country where he lives;
- To be able to read and write in languages of personal and international communication;
- To be able to provide first aid;
- To be able to cook;
- To know the structure of Earth and Nature laws;
- To know history and laws of Humanity development;
- To have a clear idea of high Ethics of people relations;
- To have an idea about works of Great Thinkers, Philosophers, Scientists, Writers, Musicians and Statesmen;
- To know examples of reasonable, rational and deadlock transformations of people's lives in Human History.

A graduate of the seventh form (14 years old) has the right to say: «I know the basic laws of Nature and high moral behaviour, I can write correctly, think, express my thoughts, provide medical assistance, go in for favourite kind of sports to maintain healthy lifestyle, dance nicely, help people, etc». It is very important for graduate to realize: «I chose the direction and type of my professional activity in a future life. I know who I want to be! ".

School of Extensive Training

With knowledge and skills of secondary education after seven year period of intense life a person can continue studying in two ways: to study at School of Extensive Training (SET) for preparation to Higher education or to get an advanced professional level of education (SVT) and have material security for decent life.

At the age of 14 pupil has quite realistic idea about the level of his ability to think and analyze the circumstances, to memorize abstract information, his creativity and real volume of knowledge of foreign languages, etc. Objective awareness of his personal qualities allows a graduate of secondary school to make an expedient decision to continue studying in 8-10 forms of School of Extensive Training (14÷17 years old).

This period can be used for thorough preparation for studying at university. For example, all high school graduates, who are going to enter universities, need necessarily a deeper knowledge of foreign languages. Also it is recommended for all to understand simple TRUTH: normal and useful direct contact with foreign colleagues is possible ONLY in CONVERSATION! No one in the world talks in written form. It is useful to study deeply the basics of mathematics, physics, chemistry and mechanics at SET for successful studying at technical specialties at university. Humanitarian specialties require in-depth preparation at humanitarian disciplines.

It is expedient to introduce into education program of 10th form a professional guidance by organization of excursions to some many companies, offices, hospitals, etc. It is enough to take one month for this useful informative process.

It is recommended to continue further development of your physical qualities to strengthen basis of future full life.

It is also necessary to take puberty into account, because girls and young men falling in love reaches its maximum at this age. This circumstance promotes development of high moral, esthetic relationships of boy and girl, and helps to develop and strengthen great Gentleman qualities in nature of young man.

It is necessary to make reorganization of Schools of Extensive Training (8÷10 classes) to give effect to all discussed circumstances and effective education forms.

By the moment of finishing high school and SET in conditions of good education system all children, teenagers and young people have already showed to other people their natural characteristics during 7-10 years of studying. Therefore teachers and schoolmates can make certain Characteristic of discovered natural gifts of school graduate, his life interests, successes in art, sport, foreign languages, etc. The document "Discovered Physical and Mental Capacities of Name" written by people who knows a person closely, will be useful to individual and his/her family in choosing future rational and effective field of working. Also it will make process of "implanting" a beginner in real conditions of work easier and more reasonable for all companies and organizations.

Moral power of teacher has particular importance to identification of God-gifted exceptional personality. Making description of characteristic features of school graduate, a teacher with deep thinking, ability of sober estimating life realities, and expert's goodwill will be able to guarantee objectivity of recommendation of all possible life ways of young person.

The Higher Education

The first university was founded in the XII century A.D. in Italy. Then, in XIV÷XV centuries many developed countries of Europe organized some state institutes. Students had tradition to visit any university by their choice and desire in different countries to listen courses of lectures and practical classes of famous teachers. All classes were held in Latin only with usage of scientific papers also in Latin. Thus, **Latin** became a universal language for communication of teachers, students and scientists independently on nationality.

The hard truth: all people on the Earth cannot read even a package leaflet without knowledge of Latin! But health care is the first duty of person! **We still don't know the true definition of notion "Competent Person" and we graduate citizens who are ignorant from the view of Mind.** It is a Shame!

As a result of speedy falling of Human morality since the XX century, nobody, even "competent scientist" does not study and does not know **Latin**. Therefore teachers and researchers **can't read** works of well-known scientists of genius in the last thousand years in **original**. But how much reasonable, useful information has been **already** said and formulated! Our contemporaries try to produce something what has already been comprehended, elaborated and written in Latin. Because of publishing modern scientific papers and textbooks in languages of every concrete country, an extremely irrational situation appeared, when the exchange of knowledge between experts of different countries becomes essentially difficult.

The development of economic and scientific relations between all countries on the Earth requires existence of effective language contact between people. For effective cooperation business people learn colloquial speech of the most civilized countries of Europe: England, France, Germany, Spain and Italy. English is the most widespread language in modern times.

Informational Education

It is strange how deep PEDAGOGICAL education can be destroying in the modern world by careless transfer to the simplified INFORMATIONAL kind of education!

At exam oral answers to clear questions in exam card were replaced by **guessing and formal proposing** of one correct answer, for example, of five (minimum) variants proposed by teacher. So anyone, even an outsider can tick accidentally, thoughtlessly the correct variant of answer and get a false positive mark for supposedly existing knowledge!

A part-time form of higher education became widespread in the XX century A.D. And some well-known, authoritative universities in Europe have unreasonable relation of students at traditional full-time and part-time forms of studying (1:10)!

Absence of Student-Teacher direct contact results in essential decrease of quality of education. Teacher's talent is worthless in our time. And it is obvious how wrong this situation is! How can be compared the quality of informational answer represented by student in writing form and a DISCUSSION, mind game with teacher! The direct contact with teacher allows student to define his real volume of knowledge, to learn how to play mind and to get worthy mark. And often, a simple tip in form of additional question allows the student to understand his wrong train of thought "of quite another story", to orient instantly and to give a correct answer. The final mark for examination of particular student will be fairly "4" or "5" instead of "2"!

It is clear to the real teachers that any **computers will not be able to replace equally a teacher** and specialist's experience, for analyzing unforeseen circumstances at present moment and drawing a conclusions of new knowledge in subject. Only a teacher can subtly, cleverly, and with taking into account student's personality natural abilities and real knowledge to prompt reasonable direction of further studying of a subject.

Everyone knows about lower level of part-time education. So according to common sense, it is expedient to liquidate part-time education in present-day volume. The part-time form can be kept only for people with physical disabilities which hinder them to move to another city or country.

What is necessary to be put in mind? Useful for human life information or unused in life knowledge, i.e. "rubbish"? What is "rational knowledge"? During the process of studying, with learning more and more new facts in chosen speciality, you became to say one thing more often: "I should learn this too, I should investigate that and that etc". As a result we have obvious paradox that the higher the level of knowledge and real qualification are, the deeper recognition comes into the brain that: "I know very little in comparison with level of possible knowledge". Such thinking stimulates to improve level and quality of speciality studying.

University Entrants Selection

Modern principle of entrant selection doesn't correspond to a reasonable basis. For example, an entrant can apply at once for five various specialities in different universities in some countries. This fact demonstrates unconcealed and shameless wish to get only "a piece of paper" in the form of diploma after four-five years studying, instead of instrument and ability to work as effectively as possible on your own natural qualities basis for interests of society and family.

Who does community need first of all? Is it 'Commentators', 'Politicians', 'Sociologists', 'Analytics' who produce nothing, or 'Sloggers' who produce goods in form of material products or mental food, who care about their health, physical development, high art, professional and humanitarian education? Why does television give the floor firstly to "talkers", who just thirst a power? Why and who needs such "professions", universities, academies, faculties? Why do so-called "statesmen" pay money to "parasitic talkers" from a pocket of workers? It is a pure demonstration of disrespect for workers!

According to specific characteristics of concrete speciality, we will look at examples of necessary rational qualities of entrant.

A person who can't stand the sight of bloody injuries or coma can't work in the field of medicine. A good memory is needed too. For example, a pharmacologist needs to have a phenomenal memory given by nature only to some people.

An ecologist, as well as a physician, should have high level of natural ability to memorize terms in Latin and rules of their usage.

And university graduate will not be successful in engineering without having inner sense, understanding of characteristics of different materials (wood, metal, plastics, etc), ability to feel laws of physics and mathematical calculations.

Person who can't stand even a smell of main elementary substances (acid, alkali, paint, etc) and can faint during classes can't be engaged in chemistry.

Textile technology is based on person's talent to understand and feel physical condition of any material or design, for example, fibres and threads in fabric, hosiery, etc.

Therefore, future expert should be able to imagine tenseness of fabric deformation process (including textile fabric), and "to revitalize" this process comparing it to living organism.

Sewing craft and manufacturing require ability to feel beauty, harmony of body proportions of person to design a product. Sewing master can't make beautiful clothes without understanding of rational balance of material characteristics and finished product purpose.

Person who can't stand even a smell of an animal, especially their excrements won't be able to work as stock-breeder.

An agrarian should love the earth, and do not perceive it as "mud", but as "wet nurse"! It is necessary to have an excellent memory to use in practice thousands known technologies of many thousands of plants and fruits.

Lawyer, besides high ability to keep in mind the exact wording of tens of thousands of Articles, should have a sense of high justice.

Many people want to work in economy. But only a small number of people are able to work effectively. Many people don't understand this. Yes, anyone can count money, but only a person with natural talent of deep reflection, arguments analyzing, imagination, and ability to formulate rational conclusions, can foresee result, look for and find the most rational, effective variant of monetary operations.

ETC.

The above-indicated requirements to natural abilities of entrant should be examined by an admittance commission at the first stage of enrolment to university. Only correspondence of entrant natural qualities to the established requirements of a specific profession allows effectiveness of higher education.

In the XX century the negative life direction of so-called civilized countries of Europe appeared, so their own productive forces, especially in labour-intensive industries, were destroyed. All laborious processes are moving to developing countries with low living standards and low-price production. Liquidation of factories and plants in civilized countries has led to loss of interest of school graduates to enter to technical universities and to study goods manufacturing. For this reason majority of entrants want to be an accountant, economist, political scientist, sociologist, etc. Easy life in excellent conditions attracts very much. But, can you really describe a situation as a fair, when a producer of goods works hard in noisy plant workshop or even outdoors under any weather conditions and lives on a minimum wage, while an accountant and a banker sit at their tables in comfortable offices and "according to the law" instant appropriate, or rather steal the property of workers with the tacit "consent" of last one! By the way, this paradox exists since old centuries. And besides, a number of graduated politicians, analysts, commentators and other "not producers" increases progressively (over 50% of total number of students) in modern universities. Why does unreasonable beginning of person triumph again?

Dear entrants, think about effectiveness of your future profession, don't submit to laziness, because CORRESPONDENCE of YOUR NATURE qualities with properties of chosen speciality will surely bring you success and pleasure in life!

Entrance Examination

For unknown reason there is a **mistrust** of knowledge assessment correctness at high school in modern practice of admission to university. And authority of Silver and Gold medals of school graduate is humbled almost to zero by institutes. It is time to stop this negative dismissive attitude to work of many teachers.

It is reasonable to provide to entrant applying for admission to university moral right to apply only for one speciality according to his personal qualities and level of knowledge. Suspension of applying for a concrete speciality is confirmed by document about 8-month of informative work at concrete company, organization or institution. It is useful to use only oral direct contact of entrant and examiner from chair of applying speciality.

Usage of modern technologies for passing entrance exams in form of written test based on GUESSING the correct answer is a demonstration of criminal Stupidity of such system founders.

The number of exams depends on characteristics of studying at concrete speciality. The subject of all exams for entrant is defined by every concrete sub-faculty and sub-faculty of foreign languages. For example, it is inexpedient to grade exams in history, geography or philology in technical universities. But exams in general engineering disciplines should be passed, for example, in mathematics, physics, chemistry, computer equipment, etc.

Educational Process at Universities

The first higher education institutions in Europe were called Universities. They provided education generally in the humanitarian disciplines: philosophy, religion, history and medicine. With development of technology there was a need to train specialists of concrete specialities. Since the XVII century the system of a concrete profession studying came to practice at universities. The fields were the following: technology, medicine, chemistry, agriculture, archaeology, pedagogy, etc.

Optimum standard of university structure was formed during its functioning (education process). For example, all students of technical university get general engineering education on the first two-three courses independently of their concrete speciality. Chairs of mathematics, physics, chemistry, theory of mechanisms and machines, machine elements, etc, use lectures and practical classes for abstract general technical education of students. Then, on this base, they provide studying of fundamentals of concrete speciality. This tradition is continued in the beginning of XXI century a. d. too.

Development of technique on the basis of numerous scientific researches allowed to amass a high level of information about some "subtleties" of technical products manufacturing. At that a necessity arises to modify technology of teaching of general disciplines in technical universities.

For example, modern general discipline (course) "Machine elements" now gives the students of concrete speciality only general abstract idea about the power analysis of cam mechanisms, kinematics and motion laws of details, velocity and accelerations diagrams, deformations of details, cycloramas, about bevel, cylindrical, epicyclic and planetary gears, about speed governors of elements of the mechanism, etc. At the practical classes standard typical mechanisms are used.

However, on looms ALL BASES of mechanics are used practically. Therefore, it is expedient and useful on "weavers" classes to study basics of mechanics on the EXAMPLES of arrangement of concrete loom mechanisms of forming fabric texture.

Let's look at the most illustrative example. At first sight it is difficult to imagine accordance and combination of two concepts: formation of fabric weave unit on a loom in educational program of course of Weaving and learning of expansion girder deformation in program of Theoretical mechanics course. However, fabric thread is a classic example of deformed expansion girder. A beam thread in weaving unit (as the girder) has two supports on two filler threads. A power load is formed by one or several wefts. Their arrangement and size can be identical or different. Thus, we have bright example for using at lectures of Theoretical Mechanics for students studying at Weaving speciality: a girder on two supports with force applied to the middle of girder or with several applied forces of identical or different strength, etc. So the effect of reasonable and wise **combination** of general technical and special **knowledge** is OBVIOUS!

Another example, it is difficult or even impossible for teacher to deform a metal detail. So, in this case it is enough to make a plastic model with one special characteristic: during its deformation some different-coloured visible areas appear exactly in the same places where force was applied. And changing the load directions we can see changing of tension locations. Thus, a teacher can demonstrate effectively various versions of load applying in real work circumstances and estimate with students structure rationality of product madden by machine-buildings.

One more important thing. It is useful to demonstrate to students some examples of physical intensity recovery of any element of detail at lectures and practical classes. For example, a teacher several times stretches slowly a thick thread and shows to students fibres behaviour, their compression, tension and limit deformation after which there is a relative offset of fibres in a thread, and a rupture of a thread. This demonstration automatically, naturally and unconsciously causes a tension of muscles in student's mind. And effect of a deep understanding of concrete speciality will reach maximum and be useful in process of future work.

This method of teaching allows to reach triple effectiveness in studying of concrete technical speciality: a deeper memorizing of mechanics laws, mechanism arrangement of studied machine and conditions of technology optimization of a concrete product type.

Education process at institutes and universities allows to discover creative students. An involvement of all students in teachers practical scientific researches, writing and defence of diploma, helps to this search. Realization of this process requires continuous development of technical basis of researches on each university chair. It is possible in the circumstances of providing good real subsidies for science in higher education institutions from the State budget.

After graduating student quite often begins to work as a teacher at the concrete company, firm or organization in order to teach, instruct and control ordinary workers knowledge. Without any teaching experience! Therefore it is time to change an attitude to a student only as teacher's listener.

In practice, education sometimes oversteps the limits of old way of studying. And against all common traditions, some creative people try to develop student skills by joining them to the Art of teaching and knowledge level controlling. For example, let's look at the two main types of classes in university: lectures and labs, and also the procedure of examination.

A teacher identifies creative student and tells him to prepare reading of one lecture. And teacher gives some consultations about work process on future lecture at needed level. During the lecture all students listen attentively to their colleague and notice his advantages, manner of speaking, quality of formulation of subject fundamentals at the lecture, fix in memory his mistakes and involuntarily automatically memorize the lecture material more thoroughly.

At the beginning of each lab a teacher usually gives a test to each student on a material of previous class. It takes a time of new lab work. As an experiment, it is recommended to teacher to appoint three students on each class (each time new people) for quality control of learning material by other students. So in the presence of the teacher students receive practical skill of a clear, accurate, but difficult process of question formulation and assessment of student knowledge irrespective of the personal relations between them. Such procedure leads students to necessity of better preparation for labs. And after carrying out all works outlined by the program the teacher himself makes final control of knowledge of all students for the purpose of better preparation to exam.

During classes each university lecturer detects especially gifted students. Therefore he can choose three most talented students in two weeks before session and propose them to organize commission for reception exams. This time is enough for the deep analysis of all materials of a concrete discipline. Practice shows, that three chosen students make full analysis of material studied at lectures, labs and practical classes again with a great desire and understanding of a high level of responsibility. Certainly, in this case, they quite often consult with their teacher to clarify their understanding of the studied subject.

Three students perform functions of examining committee at examination. And each student chooses by himself where to sit to answer after preparation of questions from the examination card: in front of the teacher or the committee. The examination student's committee makes the protocol of knowledge control indicating scores for answer to each question in the examination card and a final total score. The teacher, sitting at another table, carries out a standard examination procedure and at the same time monitors delicately three students-examiners and how they take exams. At the end of the exam, the teacher and members of the student's committee hold a joint meeting to analyze fruitfully the exam results. Of course, only the teacher puts all total scores in student's record books. The protocol of knowledge control signed by all examiners goes to the teacher too. Only standard statement with all scores signed by the teacher should be given to dean's office. As a result, a high level of Art of Student's Education is reached.

Graduate of any university receives knowledge of **the moment when** he passed exams and defence diploma. So it is possible to lag science progress very quickly in further activity. Therefore there is a need for **self-education** and the continued taking time to receive new knowledge, acquire new literature, attend exhibitions and conferences of various levels, use Internet, etc. Such processes of cognition of pedagogical art, methods of knowledge fixing on the way of **self-improvement** are useful to each person and in all spheres of life.

CHAPTER **3**

Characteristics of the Psychological Substance of Human Nature

All people are equal only at the moment of birth and at moment of the death.

It is curiously to search and discover superb zests, excellent natural quality, good deeds in profit of people, country, and humanity in person and in the history of his affairs.

In reality, there is always a combination of "Sun and Shadow", because any object, lightened with sun and brain, has light and darkened parts. What is more rational, more useful and more genteel for person to do? Is it more rational to spoil the mood of all people just due to presence of intimate defects of another person? Why are people inclined to hide, humiliate and destroy all useful and good things, made by this helpful person, and to turn him into a horrible, shameful and unnecessary person? Is it only for their own originality, the ability, supposedly, to think profoundly and objectively for publicity and glory? It is better to create something useful for people on your own, isn't it?

The history suggests that all the major natural human qualities: intelligence, thinking depth and savagery, spreaded through the world, regardless of the locality and living conditions and status of the parents to a specific position in the society. When the power is seized by wild, unmannered people who despise the aesthetic and elegant way of interacting, it mostly occurs a destruction of high moral communication rules. As a result it is formed the barbaric way of public life: the "Leader" successfully robs citizens and receives tribute without any obligations.

Manifestations of a littleness of mind, uncontrollability and adventurism practically conforming to the laws of nature can destroy not only the authority, but also human health. With a negative result it is coming disappointment of his levity. However, it is too late. Internals and brains of boxers are may be repulsed because of health risk. The authority of the man is lost inevitably when it is committed an immoral act in favour of senior management, a bribe or insolent appropriation of a public property. Ultimately, all citizens become aware of everything, and life without glory has no value for the adventurer.

In life feeling pleasure can be obtained from the mind games in the creation of useful and enjoyable affairs for people, because every good affair enhances the comfort of your own soul. So, MONEY DOESN'T BRING HAPPYNESS! Because you may have them and live in fear of it's possible losses and broil in case of unreasonable waste of money, devastation or rubbery.

Negative Human Essence

Officially, it is believed that Man is the most intelligent

creature on the Earth. So why does the humanity commits foolish actions in real life up to now (It has already been XXI century A.D.)

Race for Power

Willpower is inherent for active people. It is curiously to realize: who climbs to power and for what purpose? In real life, there are always people with the natural willpower and people with the willpower grown with someone. For this reason, it is useful to determine the level of moral qualities at first. Then it becomes clear, what a goal he established for himself: personal enrichment and satisfaction of megalomania or selfless improving of living conditions of all people of the state.

Why do people not realize the consequences of the race for power of individuals? Why do people listen and applaud to these outstanding personalities with the megalomania? Why do all the power conquerors at all levels in any state, as a rule, become rich men or millionaires? Why do citizens of any country have to vote for these individuals? Why do acting people under the power organize elections only for relevant for them disciplinable people willing to execute in full obedience all instructions "from above"? Why does the crowd not recommend for the high offices responsible people who capable to work in interests of working members of the public? Are people really used to live in helplessness? How long have people put up with humiliating disdain? And how long will this situation dominate in the world?

Of course, the history knows examples of reasonable, equitable, and humane leadership. However, modern mass media do not report about them to new generations of people. Modern rulers organize such a conscious concealment, because people immediately understand "who is who" if they compare individuals.

At all times of the dictators domination, there was a big, ruthless competition among hyperactive personalities on the assumption of the power. Working members of the public used to obey necessarily to individuals with megalomania.

So, who is guilty in actions of leaders against the people when these actions are accompanied with wild race for power and glory, self-aggrandizement, combined with internal contempt or members of the public? The answer is clear: they are simple people. They have no time, they work and live modestly without any 'crazy ideas' (they do not buy planes, islands, ocean yachts, heavy duty cars, palaces, etc.)

But once it is necessary to overcome this! Otherwise working members of the public continue to live without clean water, variety in food, decent comfortable habitation for normal (not outstanding) conditions of daily life.

Unreasonable Actions

In practice, there are reasonable and stupid operations of law can be detected in each state. Because of poor mental judgment of authors, shameful laws "inflated" with visible justice. But when they are used in real life, it often turns into public grievance because of the littleness of author's mind when they elaborate the laws.

The Stupidity is appeared primarily in people with lack of intelligence or the excessive desire to do something unreasonable. In most cases the Stupidity wins and triumphs. Why? Of course, because it is dynamic! And the intellect modestly and delicately keeps quiet in most situations of the life. This phenomenon creates the misinformation across the state.

The Wildness of the behaviour is a negative reality of life. The crowd, like a wild Stupidity, easily goes to the streets and squares, shouts, noises and requires good for people like them, and not for the majority of people of the state. It is like a whirlwind, which can carry away and destroy everything. Actions of the crowd are always adapted, cleverly and insensibly organized for the benefit of specific individuals. Then the crowd gives the impression of spontaneous procession of offended people. But this is only apparent uncontrollability. In fact actions of the crowd are controlled secretly by the intruded provocateurs in accordance with the concept of Reality Destroyer. Provocateurs hand prefabricated flags and instruments of destruction, show an example of specific wildlife actions, then the CROWD realizes the massive destruction of the reality. In the dangerous moment provocateurs embedded in the crowd are quietly disappeared and leave the crowd to take the punishment from the law enforcement. In such a way, provoked wild people can be injured and even killed.

In consequence of the degradation of people's moral portrait the negative entity of man is particularly shown at the immoral attitude to the burying process of died people. In some countries the government disposes modern municipal cemeteries on former landfills. Graves are limited to a minimum size and they are enclosed with metal fences without passage between them.(And how to approach to the grandparents and to put flowers?) It is not infrequent that bullies destroy monuments on the graves.

We can compare this with smoking. When a person begins to poison the personality of his loveless body by smoking, he deliberately, patiently and even using will power overcomes disgust, and disagreeable sensation. Then he gets used, accustoms an organism to consume a smoke instead of oxygen and not always he can show will power to refuse from the foolish destruction of his own health.

In real life, wildness (as well as stupidity) has a higher level of dynamic. In most cases it seizes power to control all spheres of public life. Why is it more dynamic and stronger? Are all enlightened and educated people weak? In reality, the majority of people want to live in civilized conditions. On this basis, the majority can easily take precedence over a wild minority. So, why do normal citizens have to accept poor living conditions?

The advantage of the wild person is in the ability of doing whatever he wants, and the well brought-up person is limited in some actions due to high moral standards. So the wild person can quickly achieve goals and become rich and even an oligarch, he derives pleasure only from material goods because moral values does not exist for him. And the well brought-up person fixes at a lower level of material security. He is always glad to show courtesy, kindness and ready to give a hand for people in need. It is pleasant for him to play his mind and to realize the achievement from the positive solution of creative tasks on advantage to all people. Such a peace of mind is unobtainable to the wild people.

All revolutions of human relations in all countries are proceed with violence against dissidents up to the execution. Leaders of revolutions are ready to kill anyone and any number of people. In their wild belief "The end justifies the means". For example, at the end of XVIII century in France and in the early XX century in Russia overactive revolutionaries with clouding of consciousness seized the power and began to exterminate noblemen of all levels as potential enemies of the people, including innocent women! In civil wars, fratricide has become the norm. So, achieving an equality of civil rights as the fair goal began to be obtained with the help of the wild barbarity! It is so simple, reasonable, decently to create equality of opportunity for all citizens on the basis of gradual and rational reformation of living conditions without violence!

The Real patriot does whatever he can for the benefit of a family and all citizens. He also aspire to have mutual respect and good relations with citizens of neighbouring countries. He does not allow himself to estrange and conflict with them.

The False patriot, as a rule, cares only about the benefits of his race. He is able to despise and humiliate people of other nationalities. Racism and Fascism were created on the basis of Nationalism. Contemporaries well know examples of the barbaric murder of millions people initiated by Europe "Leaders". For example, at the beginning of the XIX century, Napoleon decided to turn citizens of all Europe countries into French servants by force, and in the XX century Hitler made the similar decision for the benefit of the German race.

Ordinary people watch TV at home and clamour against the wild ugliness of people only in the family ambiance. On the basis of a wide TV advertising of organized protests, the false information about general actions of the citizens is appeared. There is one conclusion: the **leaders of the state satisfy minority** requirements because the support of the future Governor goes exactly from active people on elections, not from the quiet, calm, steady, respectable, high moral people. As a result, the finely organized injustice overpowers in the modern state.

In modern states it is still used the changing (rather distorting) system of the city or country NAME and even the person's name in respect to special aspects of the speech of people with the particular nationality. Although **it is clearly defined in the law that the name in any document** (especially for cash payments) **must exactly match the spelling of the name** in the birth certificate. Parents give the name to the person and nobody has the right to change it. Distortion of city names in different states are also quite common. For example, the Italian city ROMA was changed into Rim and Firenze was changed into Florence, etc. Moreover, the spelling of name and surname (especially officials) must be necessarily written in block letters with spaces between them.

In real life there are people who do not want to do something ("Let someone do, and I just look!") They only want to show off to the audience (even looking like homeless or with naked ass) and **moreover, to get money for their own amusement.** Gradually, the Human has gone on the way of transformation from working population into slackers who absorb products of other's labour. Is not it time to stop the process of raising of society pests who prone to profit by fraud and violence? Because the desire to live at the expense of others eliminates the manifestation of their own unique abilities and the disclosure of their talent for the benefit of all people.

Instead lazy life, it is useful for women to bring up children, to cognize secrets of cooking delicious food and drinks, of embroidery, weaving, cutting and sewing attractive clothes for children and relatives, to grow and process fruits, to think creatively, etc.

Instead of lazy pastime, it is useful for real men to build anything at all, to fitter, to forge useful items, to make details of wood and metal, to carry cargo, to cultivate the land, to plant trees and plants, to invent something, etc.

The meaning **"Impudence"** includes immorality, permissiveness, devil-may-care attitude to all people and moral values of the humanity. In some well-known European cities the lechery reigns quietly in Red-light districts. Shameless people are not smart enough to understand a simple truth: their wild behaviour causes not admiration but contempt with all the negative consequences in well brought-up people.

It surprises the existence on television of extensive propaganda basic traits of wild people like violence and corruption. It appears, it is a real **school** of theft, bandit attack, financial and substantive robbery. Vandals have become central figures among the crowd. As a result wild people give the discourteous people an example to follow for going from decency into brutality in all life situations. Why does not TV educates viewers about the high moral concepts like politeness, kindness, integrity, elegance, modesty, etc? Instead of this **on television the school of Mental Degradation of the Humanity is advertised!**

The reviewed examples of stagnancy and ignorance illustrate the Humanity degradation in the moral attitude. At this rate people will just dance, sing songs and arrange carnivals instead of making real goods, food, clothes. Only instilling in children a manifestation of high integrity standards will save the Humanity.

It is strange to see **paradoxical set of mind and lack of foresight.** Why do people, even with the developed ability to reflect and the games of mind ability suddenly develop and create technologies for the nature destruction and reduction of the Humanity life and of the Planet Earth life? For example, some experts with high education, or so-called 'scientists' bring enormous harm to all people by the demonstration of their poor judgment because of sincere desire to introduce necessarily into production the results of scientific research.

From the 20th century AD it has been constructing very expensive nuclear power plants to generate electricity around the world. The inevitable disruption of those always bring enormous damage to the planet Earth, because all claims of guaranteed security is lie! Why do not reputable scientists and heads of states take into account common negative possibilities of the sane (normal) man? All the people are doomed to erroneous actions, because man cannot guarantee himself the possession "iron" health and stable well-being. Hence, occurrence of inadequate actions is possible when elements of nuclear power stations are controlled. It has repeatedly led to the explosion of the entire nuclear power plant. The Control Management System stations also cannot guarantee the absolute reliability of the functioning of all numerous devices, because materials for instruments and devices have limited validity. Natural change in the physical condition of the equipment creates the factor of unpredictability of the emergency failure of any device which consists of hundreds or thousands parts. Well, why is it necessary to deceive all the Humanity? Where is the wise voice of the Nations?

The earlier heads of states and international organizations realize **the criminal using of the nuclear energy**, the sooner will be eliminated this short-sighted dangerous way of energy power delivery to the humanity, the more chances to revitalize the nature of the Earth.

And what about the dangerous coal mining with the production of the gas followed by combustion of oxygen in the atmosphere? Or process of metal production from ore, production of rolled products, blanking of heavy ship girders, airframes, car bodies. It's time to speed up significantly the substitution of metal by easily produced lightweight and durable composite materials with the internal textile reinforcing frame from heavy-duty thread (5 times stronger than steel but with the same weight). You should not wait long and realize this process slowly and quietly. It is necessary to stop the destruction of nature and the normal, natural living conditions for all flesh on the Earth because of combustion of oxygen and use of harmful ways of producing energy.

The normal man is constantly surprised by the demonstration of government's poor judgment of many "civilized" nations. Why it is necessary to invest money in super difficult, obviously dangerous ways of energy production if **simple, safe and free sources of electric energy** are known: the sun, the movement of air masses (wind), the waters of the seas and mountain streams, the temperature difference between the Earth's surface? For example, it is about time we started to work useful and rationally on the Earth: **to interchange roofs of all houses by roof-integrated solar arrays!** It is reasonable to take the capital for this business useful to all people from the fund of murder weapons creation.

Why do nobody gives publicly on television a reasonable opinion about a **necessity of interdiction of the production energy by harmful and dangerous ways? After all, stupidity is inevitably punishable as a divine retribution!** Such a deliberate progress delay of providing normal life conditions for all people (6 billion) in the world is carried out for many years only by a small group of unscrupulous and immoral oligarchs and rulers of the states (5 thousand). What a helpless ordinary people! Shame on you! Why are you not aware of your RIGHT for the reasonable management of the humanity? Are you really unable to select and approve honest, conscious, self-educated, friendly, humble personalities on the main posts of governance?

From the perspective of a normal person it is hard to imagine the need for the **wild destruction of unique architectural values of the humanity** in the conduct of endless wars. Why do modern rulers of states under the pretext of "preservation of historical values " not create conditions for the repair and restoration of the ancient architecture masterpieces as a WHOLE? And how nice it would be to use restored palaces according **to their purpose** (not only as museums)! In modern history after the Second World War it is known examples of the reconstruction of homes, palaces and church councils. For example, in Germany the ruined city of Dresden with a beautiful centuries-old architecture was restored. It's time to use such an example of reasonable and useful life.

Who needs a WAR? Does the working member of the public need to kill a complete stranger from another country and, moreover, to risk his life? Why do people need to go through the lifetime of learning the art to kill? The answer is known. Only individual rulers need to kill innocent people during the war: kings and oligarchs, in order to satisfy their wild megalomania. The new Grand Duke, the Emperor naturally uttered: Actually, we have not fought for a long time! We will be considered weaklings! It's time to prove our superiority! But why do working members of the public have to give their lives to someone, instead of their own families?

It is strikingly, but the history also testifies about useful side of wars in ancient times. For example, Alexander the Great with the conquest of the Middle East, part of Asia and Egypt established a considerable number of new cities and laid the foundation of civilization in the vast area. His successors Ptolemy and Salevk founded two powerful nations with high level of the economy. The Roman Empire expanded the civilization on large areas of Europe and provided an example for local tribes of the organization of future great states: France, Germany, Austria, Spain, etc. Conquest of America is also contributed to the formation of new states modelled on the civilized European countries.

Normal citizens wish to live with a peace of mind, quietly, silently, good for a family and other people and not to affect life of other citizens. They receive the highest moral satisfaction after planting forests, construction of (not destruction) homes, factories, bridges. But many other people, for example, walk through the woods, gather mushrooms, admire the landscape **and in theirs mind thank involuntarily unfamiliar REAL PEOPLE for planting trees!**

And what a BARBARISM to invent and produce consciously new tools for killing effectively hundreds, thousands and millions of strangers! Why do people focus their high capacity for invention of murder weapons for the benefit of personalities with the megalomania who always has guaranteed security? **Why do we need to teach normal people in killing art** or to spend huge amounts of money on weapons and troop? Why do people believe in this shameful idea: "Let's turn other people into servants in the name of our **nation**" There is a complete Barbarism! Why do all inhabitants of the planet Earth still keep silence and work on weapons factories for killing suchlike people?

The useful for people **perfect contender for the post of Manager** in the election period may reasonably be said to the public: "We are all tired of savagery, so I aspire to get power for a reasonable an useful control in all spheres of citizens' life. I know how to do it. I will not allow myself to live better than poor man in our country as long as the standard of living rises for all citizens to fully meet the necessary needs for food, health, education, upbringing, spiritual life and work.

All people on the earth live in different conditions and use different amount of words for communicating. Person, who grew up in the forest or desert, lives and will live in wild conditions. There are 200-300 words he needs to communicate with members of the tribe. It doesn't necessary for him to be able to read, write and express his simple needs in detail. When his tribe celebrates holidays, he can just stomp, tug, jump and twirl. In modern states a person, who grew up in the countryside, talks mostly with citizens only at the market selling his products. In everyday life, he begins to work on the field, on the farm and in the greenhouse at 5:00 am. At a lunch the wife serves food. Then the work is in progress again. At the evening he goes home to eat and have a rest. There is no end of such a work on the ground. He needs 500 words to communicate with people around him. It is problematic to grow up a child in a village (in the civilized sense). The television enriches the perception of new words, but these additional words are not used in everyday rural life. Young people want to move into urban living conditions for many reasons. In such a way a gradual disappearance of rural settlements happens.

Cities grow mainly due to the migration of people from rural areas. New mode of life significantly increases free time from work: work is only 8 hours a day and 5 times a week. Thus, two days off and evenings exempt for idleness! For example, in modern civilized countries it is used typical workday schedule: the work occupies 8 hours, then there is time to visit beer bar (2-4 litres of beer) with friends or acquaintances, where it is used sound sets in the form of reduced mutilated (with belching) ordinary words. Such people do not need to use a rich and beautiful language. As a result a DIALECT is appeared.

So what does the well brought up ad educated person need to do? How can we derogate speaking illiterate dialect? It turns into a negative situation: in one state, in one locality, people communicate each other like with foreigners. The difficulty of sympathy appears naturally. If rude people come to power, they immediately begin to reorganize their dialect into a new state language. As a result, a common literate citizen becomes a "foreigner"! How does it stupid and criminal to legitimize a primitive dialect instead of the rich, perfect, beautiful language of the educated people! In this case desire to improve the literacy level of many citizens disappears.

The history of the Middle Ages AD indicates the **beginning of the culture life degradation of people** in civilized Europe. For example, in the late XV century AD Columbus and his followers noticed in America many new and unusual, including the taking of smoke from burning grass. Coming back to Europe, sailors and soldiers because of long idleness on the ships began to try smoking, and overcome coughing and discomfort. At home they began to amaze friends and people around them with new original occupation.

Rich people always like to stand out among the rest. Because of idleness, they are looking for entertainments. It was they who made a significant impact on the discovery of the smoking era in Europe. So, gradually, the technology of our own lungs destruction arose and gained distribution: Smoke instead of Oxygen! In such a way the freewill wildness has spread throughout the civilized Europe, even in highly educated people, and triumphs for 500 years. The syllogism of grown rich Wreckers has been carried out from habituation of young generation to the fashionable entertainment and the "prestige" on the basis of indispenzable overcoming of unpleasant perception from smoke. Smoking parents - is a particularly deplorable example.

For some reason, amusement machines also attract people who want to get a lot of money without any difficulties. At the same time they are nervous, worry, spend family's money, and as a rule they lose (otherwise there wouldn't be a gambling business)

History suggests about repeated manifestations of a **surprising combination of mind and wildness.** However, the nature gifted the mind for man until death but wildness is eliminated (or masked) by a proper education.

Napoleon without a proper education in Corsica had megalomania and brilliant mind in the art of war. He made soldiers, who not formed and not trained properly, commanders of armies, gave them the power and aristocratic titles. As a result of victories in the XIX century AD and the killing of hundreds of thousands people, he managed to conquer many European countries. In Egypt, his wild soldiers "played" in firing from guns on the Sphinx - the historical value of the Humanity! Only immense Great Russia blitzed Napoleon's armies. In the XX century AD Hitler showed exactly the same megalomania and nationalism. Deliberate killing of innocent people has reached a fantastic value - more than 20 million. A lot of cities were practically wiped out, like Carthage by the Romans. However, Hitler's opponents also did not spare the cities of Germany. For example, U.S. bombers in one night destroyed an entire city - Dresden, cultural heritage of the humanity. And at the end of war they dumped nuclear bombs on two peaceful cities of Japan. Again hundreds of thousands innocent people were killed. It is sad to remember these facts, but history is history, it cannot be changed.

The hope for reasonable, pleasant and beautiful life of humanity, progress of human values, is occurred repeatedly in a history known to contemporaries. However, a falling of moral values, fair, reasonable, useful norms of people's life occasionally happened and are happening, especially in the XXI century AD. This tendency is clearly illustrated in **Fig.1** as a subjective **schedule of level change of Humanity's morality from the eighth century BC to the twenty-first century AD.**

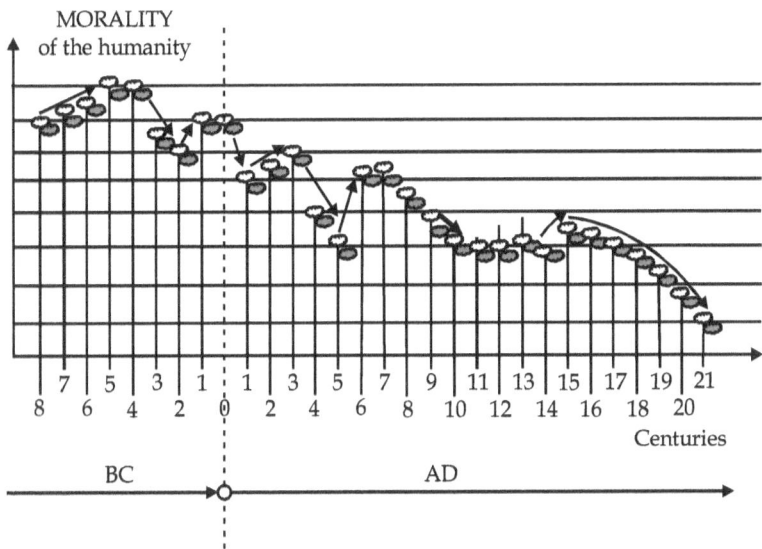

Fig. 1: Level change of Humanity's morality over the past 29 centuries

The construction of this schedule is executed on the basis of recognition of outstanding acts of great thinkers and statesmen. For example, in the **eighth** century BC Lycurgus accurately formulated "Rules of human conduct".

In the **seventh**, and then in the **sixth** centuries BC Solon genius formulated and introduced something that would be useful for us to use in the period of creation of future uniform state "People of Earth". For example, the earth and the personality were appeared free from debts, the jury was entered, and the political will of the people began to be expressed by people's assembly of all adults. It is surprisingly: the poor and the rich acquired the equal rights! And IT was offered and used in the sixth century BC! The sixth century B.C. also presented to the world great thinkers - Pythagoras, Heraclitus and Aeschylus.

The **fifth** century BC is justly called "The Golden Age of Humanity development". For example, Pericles, Phidias, Anaxagoras, Sophocles, Herodotus, Protagoras, Socrates, etc, provided to the world Beauty of Athens, Wisdom, High Art, Virtue, History of events and wars. Hippocrates founded the doctrine about Medicine, and Confucius designated the necessity of good relations in a family, love to younger and devotion to seniors.

The **fourth** century BC became famous for Plato, Aristotle and Epicurus outstanding works, the spreader of a civilization Alexander the Great, etc.

In the **third** century BC Epicurus planned a way to the serenity of mind, and Archimedes presented to the Humanity basic laws of mechanics.

In the **second** century BC Polybius provided to the Humanity the first general history of society development and recommended the use of a reasonable combination of a monarchy, aristocratism and democracy.

The **first** century BC was filled a second time with events and pieces of art of international standard. Cicero, Lucretius, Gaius Julius Caesar, Publius Vergilius Maro, Quintus Horatius Flaccus, Publius Ovidius Naso, Maecenas and others have provided to the Humanity for all times pieces of art and examples of the high moral relations between people.

During the new era it was observed a gradual decrease in level of Humanity's morality. This is shown by widely known numerous descriptions of historical events and life of special personalities.

From the **15th century AD** and up to now it is observed the steady and intensive (without significant level of fluctuations) tendency of falling of the moral relations between people on a planet Earth. Surprisingly, but this FALLING of morality is accompanied by the same level of intensity of INCREASING a level of equipment development! Well, why did it happen? Why did the development of technology began to destroy in world wars tens of millions innocent citizens? The answer is one: **the development of a freedom of actions of rich people to level of PERMISSIVENESS led to MORALS destruction as concepts!** As a result, even today there is a danger of destruction of life conditions by means of destruction of the atmosphere and all alive for all the inhabitants of the planet Earth.

Further it doesn't make sense to suffer this global situation. Destruction of useful natural resources can lead to death of the Humanity and elimination of all alive on the Earth. The Work of God who found in the Universe one planet 'Earth' with suitable conditions for the rational organization of life for all flesh, can be vain! That is why **there came a critical time in the understanding by all people that it is necessary to refuse tribal and nationalist organization of all kinds of states in the world and useful organization of the one single state "EARTH"!**

Positive human essence

The God awarded Humanity unique feeling of LOVE for the neighbour. It is so fine and incomparable! This wonderful high phenomenon of sincere expression doesn't demand an explanation. **And the Soul of the Person is treasure in each of us. It is touching, lovely, charming!** The need for love to the person and from the person is always existed and will exist. It is pleasant to bring a benefit to all alive and to all nature on Earth.

Let us try to remember such an accurate, clear sayings about reasonable actions of the person which were formulated in Latin proverbs long ago:

- The obvious doesn't need the proof;
- The truth can be helpless, but never perishes;
- Nonsense – mother of all troubles;
- The fool can deny more, than the philosopher can prove;
- Reasonable silence is better than foolish talk;
- The criticism has to be free from slander;
- Clever person approves nothing without proof;
- Clever person never becomes presumptuous;
- Wisdom is an eye of life;
- Laws can't bring benefit where there is no moral;
- The highest law is the benefit of all people;
- Mind is the soul of the law;
- It is hard to rule over others if you aren't able to direct yourself;
- The deep rivers of reason flow with a smaller noise.

In modern life it is possible to establish the astonishing fact of a contradiction and injustice. For example, useful, pleasant qualities of the person, such as kindness, honesty, decency, good breeding, etc, turn into shackles of inadaptability of an individual to the manifestation and influence of negative rather wild realities of life!

Worthy Character Traits of the Person

The MODESTY doesn't prevent other people to live. The simple, normal, natural person doesn't dare to live at the expense of others because HE can't do otherwise. He doesn't need to impose his talents. HE does not seek to specify, to command to people to do just as he wishes. HE doesn't climb to power or domination. Surrounding people in acknowledgement of his high qualities can ask him to operate them, rather **coordinate** cleverly and effectively their actions with reasonable hope for benefit in life. Such a trust to MIND, DECENCY can naturally lead to consent to hold the post of the Managing director by actions of group of people in any number.

Why does the Worthy person live quietly and without self-advertisement? Because, he is satisfied with consciousness of the abilities to creativity. He quietly does his work with all the heart and wishes to be quite often the Hermit because privacy gives a freedom of reflections without external intervention of everyday life realities.

Newcomer engineer is usually modest in reflections and doesn't wish to think about the solution of a fundamental task. This normal occurrence interferes the identification of talent which he doesn't suspect. It doesn't reasonable for people to hide USEFUL. Therefore sensible person with operated modesty only waits for an opportunity and cleverly, unassumingly creates and organizes the conditions for involuntary manifestation of attention to results of his useful affairs or innovative ideas from surrounding people (not on his personality).

During the games of mind or reflections it is reasonable to ask yourself an enlighten question: **"Why do earlier celebrated personalities acknowledged by the history, have to be OBLIGATORY cleverer us?"** Are we, modern people, were degenerated as speculating personalities? The known thousand-year history of the Humanity testifies that the Most High God constantly disseminates from above talents and property for deep speculations. Only 'Rulers' notice seldom this phenomenon because anybody can't be (allegedly) cleverer and more capable than they. Thanks to Thinkers who managed to publish the works for using by future generations during lifetime.

In real life it is used the negative rule of doubt in usefulness of deep reflections of the gifted personality. However, where can be the harm in advancing the time by "airy fairy" outstanding thinkers? It would be useful to use the simple reasonable rule of life in practice by surrounding people: to exempt gifted Thinkers from usual cares for using **irreplaceable time** for the Humanity benefit. This action isn't megalomania underlining, it is just understanding of real actual, useful features of this Personality.

GOODWILL, RESPONSIVENESS, RESPECTABILITY are always useful for all people.

The man of virtue not only sympathizes with a grief of other person, wishes well to him and takes a detached view of use of its wish, but also tries to make something useful for him and his family.

In the V century BC the philosopher Protagoras uttered briefly and volumetrically: "Virtue is the best moral condition of the person". Really, the good creates high peace of mind.

The normal Person is in a possession of natural desire to provide a meal for all family members, to take care about their health, to create all useful conditions of a life and to offend nobody. The normal person is not concerned at all about skin, hair and eyes colour, a nationality of the stranger in the unknown to him district, he isn't able to afford to carry out something that will bring damage to another. Intellectuals respect in advance all strangers, wish well and health to them, they are always glad to help them with difficulties and to express a wish: "May God give you the Human Happiness!". It is enough not to ignore people's natural simple requests so that their lives are not been interfered. The normal person always derives pleasure from the help to the neighbour, to the colleague and to the stranger. Freedom of Kindness

Manifestation Has no Restrictions! It is so PLEASINGLY to ENJOY the JOYFULNESS of OTHER PEOPLE!

In real life all people with normal living conditions can give a help to relatives, to acquaintances and to strangers in case of need, because people understand the simple truth: they can appear in the future in a similar situation (a fire, an accident, a grabbing, etc). The help to another is it's so nice for the Soul! Even greedy, envious, impudent thieves and bandits by nature can get to situations of manifestation of good, for example, to their child, their beloved, their mother, etc.

The belief in force, power, prettiness, appreciation, indisputability, efficiency, beauty of GOOD for all people on the Earth brings a powerful charge of energy into own heart and soul. The kind act always inspires for useful acts you didn't venture earlier. It turns out the beautiful chain of spontaneous manifestation of good. It is so fine in every respect!

The POLITENESS is treated unambiguously at first sight. However in practice politeness has various forms of manifestation: Benevolent, Delicate, Immaculate, Official, Deliberate, Demonstrative, Artificial, Counterfeit, Visible.

How to deal with that fact if you want to tell the truth to other person? The inconsistent situation turns out: it is impossible to distort the truth, but the polite truth can be "bitter" and capable to bring to the interlocutor a psychological trauma. Thus, not always it is possible to be polite from a position of concept "Truth". In this situation it is useful to arrange previously a conversation form: diplomatic, delicate or frank 'mannishly', with an exposition of the thoughts in strict accordance with the concept "Truth", i.e., frankly, but without the offence, polite with quiet perception of the interlocutor (if he wishes).

CONSCIENCE is very valuable quality of person's nature. It is expressed in compassion to the injured person, the feeling fear of doing the harm to people, understanding of need to correct casual bad own acts and to fill damage with the victim.

SINCERITY allows emotions to be shown from within with full frankness without considering of consequences. This quality contains pleasant action for perception. However, it also can do a harm to the person. Therefore it is desirable to accustom yourself to a fast preliminary estimate of circumstances.

The SELF-RESPECT allows the well-mannered person to keep the independence and not to allow humiliating actions on people surrounding him. The result is an involuntary respect of people for his results. For example, the young Roman soldier Muzio Scaevola convincingly showed the will power, controllability, fearlessness, nobility, self-respect to the Etruscan emperor Porsenna in Ancient Italy (497 year BC). During the interrogation he lowered the hand into the campfire before Porsenna and didn't make any noise as a sign of fearlessness before executions. Clever Porsenna was amazed and delighted with Muzio's act, that is why he called off the execution and concluded with Romans a peace with honour.

Harmony of the Actions

What is the EQUALITY in life? Whether it can be? Will people ever be equal? In what it can be?

It is time to understand, realize the simple truth: all people are differ in their natural physique and mental abilities. It is notorious that various talents are gifted to different people by the Almighty! Depending on thinking level all people understand and treat the basic concepts of life, for example, justice, in their own way. In the presence of this natural objective circumstance to be guided by subjective understanding "Equality in everything and for everyone" is profound, superficial delusion which does not reflect reality of being!

It is one undeniable truth: the actual inequality of levels of a physical condition of the organism and mental abilities of person will remain also in the future of Humankind. Despite this fact, equality NEEDS to be observed in many fields of activity of all people on the Earth. For example, all people have the moral right for elementary necessary living conditions, for elementary and general education to work for the good of family.

The higher education is objectively available only to people with high level of mental abilities. For, what is the point to show the desire to become physicist or mathematician if you are not capable to reflect abstractly at sufficient level? "The Human History" also demands the existence of ability to deep objective reflection and analysis of accomplished events. **You should not wish that that does not correspond to your nature**. This is a useful starting position of intelligent human life. And still **there is an absolute Equality** on the planet Earth: ALL living beings are born and die.

The word FREEDOM attracts all people. This is the fact. The permissiveness can really be shown when a person lives alone in the forest, mountains and desert. Do what you want and as you want! It is not necessary to spend time thinking about the consequences. This is wild use of the concept THE FREEDOM.

In real life, person lives surrounded by other people. Everyone wants to satisfy his/her requirements according to individual abilities and needs of an organism. However, he has to take into account the objective situation of cohabitation with similar people. Here person cannot do without brain activity. It is necessary to think: "What will family, friends, colleagues think about my act? Will it be pleasant or awful, useful or harmful for them?" Only after the analysis of possible consequences it is necessary to make a final decision about the further actions. Certainly, this process needs some time that is not always desirable.

For some reason the majority of people, without thinking, find it possible to live in COMPLETE freedom of their actions because only then (in their opinion) there will be a democracy in the state. Actually this delusion is a demonstration of superficial thinking "not above a nose".

Can the FREEDOM be absolute? Of course not! Even animals are limited to actions of other creatures. And people? That is why in any society it is advizable to create clear rules of behaviour of each person at home, on the street, at work, on the nature. For their observance it is necessary to bring up the manifestation of controllability of their behaviour with self-respect observance since the childhood. This is the reality of life.

We live by ourselves. That is why we must arrange well conditions of our life (housing, roads, surrounding reality) in the minimally required volume by OURSELVES. For some reason in real modernity an amazing irrational circumstance dominates: in cities everyone got used to laziness (even with hardworking nature) and to obligatory service by the abstract "state". For example, a worker of housing and communal department supposedly has to make emergency repair of the roof, water pipes and basement of a house in the city. But he is busy with other work or has no necessary material. People as helpless beings are waiting and waiting for an abstract worker. So, should we quietly watch the water leak on ceiling of the apartment? The simple principle of behaviour that is useful for normal balanced life: IF I CAN I WILL DO IT MYSELF without any reward. For example, is it really difficult for normal man to buy one roll of covering, to climb immediately on a roof and repair the damaged place? THANKS will be told automatically from all surrounding people for the benefit of his sincere pleasure and authority! And who spoils elevators, walls of stair flight and doorway, yard and children's playgrounds? Who throws garbage wherever he wants? Of course, it is hard-working, but ill-mannered people.

The Conclusion: it is our fault, we should work and keep order for own benefit, for family and neighbours by ourselves.

JUSTICE is what is reasonable, what is born by reason, instead of momentary mood. At first, you need to think, to estimate everything, to find a rational and fair solution of a problem. Justice will never bring harm to ordinary citizens therefore justice is a basis of creation of the reasonable, useful relations of people in any mini-state.

Up until now, all communities of people are subdivided into rich and poor, workers and managing directors, producers of material and spiritual values and those who appropriates them as the chief, statesman, etc. This fact is truly depicted on the caricature in the XIX century: "**One** Working Man **with a PLOUGH, Seven** Spongers **with a SPOON!**"

There are a lot of professions of Sponging: speculators, talkative commentators, politicians, jobbers, controllers, etc. An increasing number of such "experts" count other people's money and "glued" most of them to themselves.

In reviewing the rules of reasonable, benevolent communication of people of this state firstly you should distinctly, clearly, comprehensibly, understandably formulate and prove correctness of useful high ideals of human communication (ethics) and not the low human needs. The observance of high moral rules of cohabitation should provide the Restriction of Freedom to show low wild instincts. It is already time to show hot aspiration to justice.

Mind and Reason

The Mind of all beings controls their actions. It is capable to estimate the real circumstances and to make the decision on the concrete necessary act. However, even the great Mind can be limited from objectivity by a partition or "curtain" and to bring only desirable commands to actions.

The Reason is the Mind capable to estimate many objective circumstances and to draw real conclusions with a minimal level of restrictions. Possibilities of Reason are huge! Practically it has no real circumstances, problems which it will not be able to comprehend and find unexpected, innovative, simple, obvious solution for the benefit of case and person. The common sense solves all problems!

The aura of thoughts and spirit energy is formed around the human nature in the process of thinking. This invisible cover protects the person from many negative impacts of environment!

It is effective to use Ñonsciousness and Subconsciousness for productive impact on the interlocutor. For example, we try to achieve the goal by presenting strong arguments and evidences. The interlocutor states the arguments with substantiation of real negative circumstances. The result is refusal in your request, offer and case. If you will find arguments of impact on interlocutor's subconsciousness, then your substantiation of necessity of solving the problem at the level of the sum of Consciousness and Subconsciousness will allow to connect the interlocutor's natural abilities and emotions. As a result in the interlocutor's mind the search of positive substantiation of necessity of solving this problem and elimination of problematic states of the case will start. It is useful to turn "Minus" into "Plus"!

It is reasonable to develop the art how to say so that nobody will be able to disprove your arguments. As a result it is useful and effective, practically since the beginning of conversation to address to mind and to internal, fine, inspiring, positive emotions of own nature. Then THIS will pass to the interlocutor and the task set by you will be solved positively for the benefit of people with his help.

See for yourself. It is a bright, well-known example. The drunk aristocrat made a bet: "I can drink the sea. If I will not drink it, then all my fortune will be yours". In the morning he woke up and clutched his head: "I will be a beggar now!". And then the true Great Mind of the Wise Servant suggested to the master a simple ingenious way out from the deadlock: «Make a condition to your friends: "At first dammed all rivers flowing into the sea, only then I will drink it! "».

This shows that you should never panic, give up and regret about impossibility to solve a difficult problem. It is useful to unite Reason and Persistence and in deep, calm, businesslike and as if in abstract way to reflect on many variants of search of a major factor of the positive solution of the problem. And trifles will be solved then by themselves.

Practice of life developed effective process of time-saving for considering of typical actions of individual. For this purpose it is necessary to think over the typical situations of life and to put THE RULES OF LIFE into your brain. It will allow to make the decision quicker and rationally react on facts of life at the right time.

It is surprising, why do smart people give the power and obey to wild, unruly people? Where is the justice? Why do smart people often weak in acts? Where is their manifestation of self-esteem and desire to carry out actions useful to simple people? It is obvious demonstration of weak character and excessive tolerance, because in real life the combination of high level of mind with negative qualities of human nature is often observed, for example, with uncontrollability in acts and indecision.

"Curtained" Mind

Almost the majority of people on the Earth were limited by the Almighty in mental abilities since birth. Therefore, for certain individuals with small restriction it is hard to live among intellectually curtained people who do not understand the obvious and simple.

For the curtained person Truth is what is favourable, desirable to him that is why he takes only those evidences which confirm his prejudices.

The smart person subtly and clearly outlined the contradictory actions of people in modern states: "**The Swan – the Crayfish – the Pike**". Each creature pulls the fruit in its own direction: to the sky, on the ground, to the water. As a result the fruit remains on a place. It means that, any significant problem of life cannot be solved without the possibility of coordination of actions by creatures with essentially various ways of life.

In practice daily rules of life are formed only by individuals at the power. Their mental limitation is quickly detected when real negative and dangerous situations appear in life.

For example, guaranteed obstruction of traffic through a railway track is provided by using barrier which was invented a long time ago. However, many railway crossings are still used only restrictive side signs which do not prevent crazy drivers to cross railway tracks in front of a moving train. That is why every year in many countries people die in buses and ordinary cars. And what about violation of the elementary traffic rules when drivers overtake with a mad speed and enter the contraflow lane? Every day many thousands of innocent people in the world die because of impatient savages. Therefore, it is time to improve the state foundation – moral of behaviour, self-controllability, respect and observance of rules of safe life.

The typical reactions of people to the simple, obvious solution of a complex problem are: "What is new here?", "I also can do so!", "It is plain as day!", "It is too simple!", "There is nothing to pay for!". Person is lazy to think that: yes, he sees this with his eyes but does not realize this by reason (i.e. does not see). He does not have enough mind to understand that such answer shows his narrowness of thinking, inaptitude or inability to think logically and formulate a rational conclusion.

For example, Columbus at the end of the XV century AD was convinced in the opening of new land, continent "America". At the end of the report the humiliating remark was made to the King of Spain Ferdinand Columbus: "There is nothing special, new, difficult and outstanding in your proof of the fact of discovery of New Land". Then Columbus suggested all present grandees to put an egg on a table. Many tried, but nobody could make it. Then Columbus with easy blow put the egg on the table by flattening of its top. That was a moment when nobles said the still alive phrase: "There is nothing new, anyone is able to do this!".

Only the smart Person will worthily estimate such actions: "It is ingeniously simple!", "You are the Genius!". Really, nobody will be able to throw into question the reality of an embodiment of ingenious thought!

Let's review the examples of obvious paradox.

In practice it is used the reasonable principle of the solution of all problems by specific experts. However, their imagination is limited by professional knowledge. They "exactly" know what is necessary and what is not necessary to do. As a result, inconvenient in operation devices, mechanisms and machines are quite often made. For example, before adjusting one device in the mechanism, it is necessary to dismantle another.

The well-known modern car is a striking example of thoughtlessness of experts. For example, inner tubes, which easily pierce with a sharp object on the road during the motion, are still used in tires. Thousands of people die every year. There are still used side mirrors with limited vision of situation on the road, while the video cameras on the rear window were developed long time ago. Light vehicles transformed into load-carrying vehicles by increasing of external size of the boot which is filled completely only in case of a trip to the summer cottage or to another city. Such cargo boot distorts, spoils an external aesthetic image of the car and prevents designers to achieve beautiful, refined, excellent forms of a harmonious combination of proportions of constituent elements. Such "load-carrying vehicles" are "working horses", and not "light vehicles" for pleasure of people with natural property to feel everything beautiful in surrounding reality.

Paradoxically but it is useful to listen to opinion of the clever novice without experience. He knows exactly what he needs for ease of use, physical and mental comfort. He still does not know that it is impossible to do so. That is why the novice with high level of game of mind can propose the **innovative, simple** solution of a technical problem which will not come to mind to the competent expert!

Limitation's Variety of the Mental Capacity

In the further analysis of limitation of mental capacities of the person or rather his outlook, width of view on the world, thinking depth, it is convenient to use such conditional concept as Curtained on the basis of two similar concepts: "Blind" and "Curtain". The Almighty gives to the child from his birth only the initial position of blinds and curtain concerning a source of sight (thinking).

The blinds limit person's "averted vision", "close" person's eyes to something beyond the blinds.

The curtain limits the depth of diffusion of vision between curtains.

The Blind and the Curtain can have different level of transparency: from semitransparent to opaque. Therefore they isolate the brain from reality with various degree of intensity.

In general, there are three directions in which the curtained mind is shown: in a breadth of vision of the facts of life, depth of thinking and height of an initial position when assessing the development of events.

All people are born with brains of about the same volume. However, mental capacities are limited in varying degrees because the blinds and curtains presented by the nature have various intensity (density) of blackout (transparency), different length **L** limitation of view and thinking, and also disclosure at different angle a **(Fig. 2).**

Child's blinds and curtains are light, semitransparent and easily draw apart. It is necessary only to help him to draw them apart. In time, with age, blinds and curtains become hard, darker and low-permeable. It is more difficult to draw them apart and look round, to see surrounding reality, to estimate a real situation in life. The earlier a person starts to draw them apart the quicker and better learns world around.

The more the angle of disclosure of reflections α is, the wider the outlook of "game" of mind is. The more the length of L blinds is, the farther the front curtain is placed from the person's head, the more the depth of review is, the further the understanding of reality and mind game extend while analyzing the reality of life.

The angle of disclosure of blinds is determined not only by natural data. In further life with high level of upbringing, education and self-education it is possible to draw blinds apart (α) and to increase their length **(L)**. Finally, the increase of **breadth and depth of thinking** will allow to discover and learn your natural abilities and talents. Life will be surely more interesting and fruitful!

On **Fig. 2** four variants of thinking are presented: in the breadth α_i of disclosure of side blinds and depth Li of arrangement of a front curtain:

1. $L_1 = L_2$ and a1 > α_2;
2. $L_5 > L4 > L_3$ and α_3 = Const;
3. $L_7 > \rightarrow L_6$ and $\alpha_4 > \rightarrow \alpha_5$;
4. L_8 Max and α_6 Max.

Different people have different angle of disclosure of blinds $\alpha_1 \alpha_2$, with the same depth of thinking $L_1 = L_2$.

The Outlook and Breadth of thinking are measured by the angle ai which can be increased by serious education and broadening of outlook of real life. This requires work, work and awareness of need for constant self-education.

The Depth of thinking Li is defined and put into brains by Mother Nature. It is convenient and easy for normal person to see within eyesight. But to see does not mean to realize, to understand essence, significance, usefulness and prospective of implementation of the seen. Therefore such well known saying appeared: "He cannot see beyond his nose!".

The person cannot increase a natural maximum L_{max} given by the Almighty! It is useful to reconcile with this objective circumstance. The realization of the mental abilities will allow person to build reasonably the education and the useful practical activity in the atmosphere of inward peace.

It is useful to consider such important fact: different people with the same natural value L_{max} can practically use different values L_i. In reality there are few who can reach the L_{max} by a hard work in the process of education. The one, who does not have diligence and is not "workaholic", will never reach the greatest possible depth of thinking, given by the Almighty.

In practice of being one more measurement for an assessment of events development is used: from the height of starting position. For example, the buildings in the city restrict conditionally the distance (depth) L_i and the viewing angle β_i in the vertical plane. When thinking (conditionally) from height of clouds the distance L_i and the viewing angle β_i naturally increase by hundred or thousand times.

"Hovering in the clouds" is peculiar to far-sighted personalities with the high level of imagination and mind. On the modern Earth the Mind is covered with low dense clouds of Nonsense. It is a problem to break through them! Therefore the high Mind rises into clouds and on the top looks for gaps among the Gloom of Wildness and Limitations of Mind.

Analogy: the "normal" person goes on the street of the city and sees only within the direct area restricted by houses. The person who rise in clouds sees many times farther therefore it is easier for him to foresee a real situation on the whole route and to predict possible events. However, in practice of being, the Person who profoundly thinks about perspective of a concrete way in life is often perceived by other people as the person not capable to see real life. The surrounding people consider his thoughts as unnecessary therefore they do not perceive them for implementation. Such typical judgments hinder the development of the whole society of people.

If the person really likes something, he is ready to learn this without limitations on the scope of necessary work. Such purposefulness is usually implemented by self-education, performance of experiment with the following analysis of results, formulation of conclusions and identifying of further work for satisfaction of vital interests.

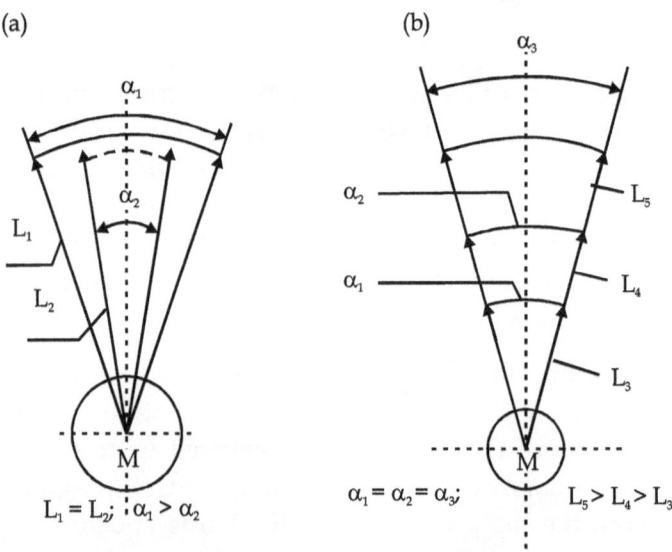

(c)   (d)

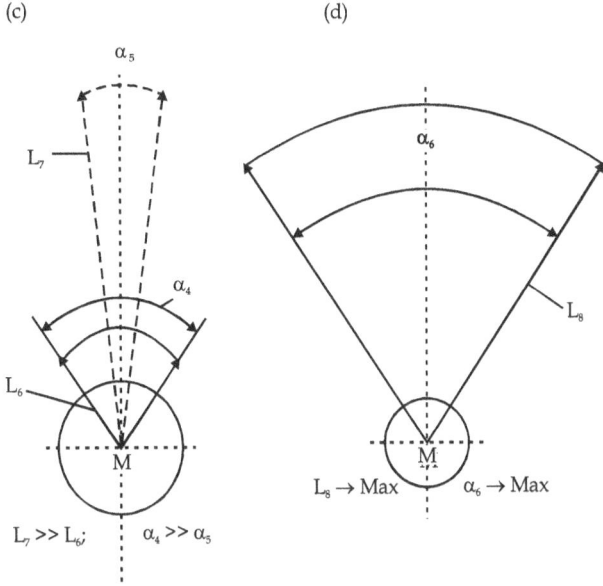

Fig. 2: Variants of curtained mind in depth Li and breadth ái of reflection

It is considered that if professor has a rank "professor", "scientist", the author is automatically associated with literacy in all fields of activity. This delusion does not consider his natural human qualities, for example, presence or absence of benevolence, decency, natural politeness, megalomania, greed, etc.

In real life the future professor can grow up in a family of ill-bred people with negative natural qualities which can get into nature of future scientist in the childhood and youthhood.

With luck, such "child" can get to a surrounding of people from normal families, graduate, finish postgraduate study and defend the dissertation. Here it is not necessary to confuse two types of activity: carrying out scientific researches and manifestation of qualities of nature. Scientific researches can be conducted at very high level, and high ethics of the people's relations depend on level of imitation to people with the high level of education. Not always such a person can become the real Intellectual.

Let's consider the common examples of combination of high knowledge in specific specialty and negative consequences of absence of normal education of outstanding scientists.

Medical worker- professor, the specialist in treatment of a specific human disease will certainly be able to find symptoms of this disease at any patient and to prescribe a course of treatment. However, the use of specific modern effective drugs can bring harm to other human organs.

Nuclear power industry scientists devote their activities to dangerous researches of an atomic structure of a matter. At first sight this is fair and reasonable (from their subjective point of view). All scientists, manufacturers, statesmen publicly assert about the complete safety of nuclear power plants. And what is the result? Still there are disasters, loss of many thousands of people, damage to the nature. Is not it a shame to you, misters "good"?

Curtained Vanity brings great damage to the world.

And still, it is useful and rational to give the floor to the reasonable Thinker who possesses a combination of rare qualities of the person:

- thinking depth "below a sea bottom";
- the ability to clearly, distinctly, understandably formulate thoughts, ideas and recommendations;
- the ability to provide proofs which nobody will be able to refute;

- the independence of opinions without pleasing to someone;

- sufficient courage before possible, dangerous counteraction of masters of the modern life;

- absence of aspiration to indispenzable enrichment at the expense of other people;

- intolerance of living conditions which are unworthy of Person;

- benevolence;

- the ability to work quietly, without advertising, decently; etc.

The Thinker is able to effectively participate in the conversation: "A Silly question - a Real Answer - a Reasonable Solution".

Truth Tree

The earth should be fertilized and watered when planting a tree. It is necessary to take care of the tree permanently that it firmly got accustomed. For example, it is necessary to "feed" it permanently with water, to pollard for growth facilitation with rational layout of branches for fruits and beauty. The tree can die without proper care. This is an example of how people should take care of reasonable sequence of actions to resolve any life problems.

Root of all Problems

The tree and floating flower on water can be used as illustrative full-fledged ANALOGUES of process of rational thinking of person.

What is primary, and what is the consequence, what is the most important and main for satisfaction of vital needs of water plant and tree?

Fig. 3 shows images of water plant **(a)** and tree **(b)** from root to flower on the water and the top of a tree trunk.

Clearly visible floating plant on the water surface **(Fig. 3, a)** is the illustrative analogy of short-sightness of thinking. Surprisingly, the majority of ordinary people see only a beautiful flower on water. Ordinary people are not interested in what gave rise to this flower, how the trunk of flower lives in water what construction it has.

Curious people also pay attention to a trunk under water: what is its structure, single or branched, etc. Profoundly thinking person will dive into the water, dig out the bottom and learn the root structure, the principle and strength of its fixing in soil, the measure of stability of all plant. Besides, the person learns also the matter of bottom soil and measure of its productivity.

Thus, it is possible to define three variants of depth of touch of reality and thinking of the person:

- on a water surface (flower),
- in the depth of water (stem),
- at the bottom and in the bottom (root).

Can the water flower appear without the stem? Usually, No! Can the stem appear without root? No! The Conclusion: **The foundation of the plant is the Root in the bottom of the pond.**

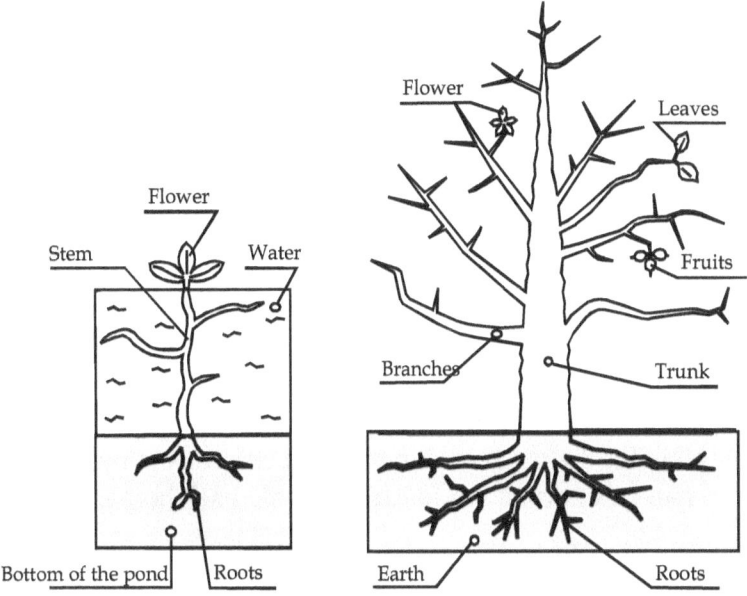

Fig. 3: Images of Structures of a water plant (a) and tree (b).

The ROOT **(Fig. 3, b)** revitalizes a tree after hibernation, takes moisture from the earth and feeds a trunk, branches, leaves, flowers and fruits with the **purest juice**. While the root is alive, the trunk grows, and fruits ripen for reproduction of new trees. In its turn, the leaves absorb nutrients from the atmosphere and feed branches, trunk and roots. This is the interaction of all parts of the tree.

In real life only appearance of a tree attracts the majority of people therefore they can (without considering the consequences) quietly cover with asphalt the earth under a tree for placement of seats, etc. As a result roots suffocate and the tree dies slowly. In the same way, the material, physical and mental well-being of people on the Mother-Earth depends on a status of a moral basis of human life (the Root of Life).

In life of the modern state The Rulers are mainly busy with the Leaves of the Problem Tree: clean leaves, inhale aroma of flowers and eat fruits. The root is not visible to them in the earth and therefore they do not pay attention to it (however know about its existence). But there are a lot of leaves, flowers and fruits on the Tree! And they change every year! Therefore the Rulers of the state do not have time to ennoble the foundation, the source of all problems. And nobody wants to realize This. If it is not necessary to spend forces and effort for manifestation of stupidity and immorality then the knowledge, establishing and adhering of the reasonable civilized principles of moral require additional efforts and restrictions in behaviour. It is easy to throw on the street an ice cream label or a piece of paper, a bottle in the forest, etc. A problem for the modern ill-mannered citizen is to put a piece of paper in a pocket and to carry a bottle back home!

The simple truth: any state, without proper attention, daily care of condition and development of the life foundation – the MORAL, is doomed to loss. Elimination of all wild realities of life is possible only by continuous development of high moral qualities of the person.

Television willingly shows scandal stories, crime stories with murders, wild discussions of politicians with fights, bribery, etc. It is no time for examples of manifestation of good, training of delicate communication manners ("There is no popularity!"). Is it so difficult to understand a simple truth: only the increase in number of citizens of high moral will reduce the number of criminal offences and create the soil for growth of prosperity of all simple workers. Therefore it is useful for all citizens to create the Reasonable Government, capable to get to the Root of problems.

Wisdom

The Wise man is able to find a zest in the ocean of philosophical meditations. Monumentality of his reflections affects our imagination. The thought of the Wise man is tremendous, deep and mysterious. It goes ahead of this era and is never mistaken.

There are few people who can "get to the Root" of any phenomenon, reflect deeply and logically and make useful conclusions. Wise advice, as a rule, are always contains optimum conditions of implementation of rational person's actions, **because the Wise Man looks now and sees that will be in the Prospect!** For this purpose it rises to the Clouds of Future World.

Certain outstanding personalities, in process of gaining of life experience, significantly draw apart curtains of thinking and look far into the future without restriction of "game of mind". As a result, begins the moment of realization of fundamental laws of life on the nature and fixing of unique property of nature to see the obvious. The wise man understands that there is no opportunity to correct the ethics of all people quickly during lifetime of this generation therefore he should be guided only by future generations of people. At the last stage of the life he wishes to stay alone, not to disturb others and quietly reflect in peace of mind. In the first century BC the philosopher and writer Titus Lucretius Carus define the ideal of the wise man in the poem "On the Nature of Things".

Intravital recognition of wisdom of the person happens very seldom and only after creation of significant cases. But to achieve this, you need to spend a lot of effort and years of life for everyday existence. Where get funds for this? As a rule, the wise men do not consider the material luxury as main goal of life and do not strive for power in a society of people with the low level of civilization. It is time to refuse the practice of intravital ignoring of the rarest gift of Nature – Human Wisdom. Because, the earlier the wisdom recognition will come, the more benefit it can bring to Humankind.

Many thousands of Princes, Emperors, Presidents, Shahs, Sultans, etc. ruled the states. Whose names remained in the History and Memories of the modern people? We know the names only of some outstanding statesmen. In a bigger measure the names of Creative Personalities have remained in the Human history and in people's memory, the names of philosophers, historians, inventors, sculptors, artists, musicians, etc. In the modern world the enormous states funds are immediately spent for entertainments, instead of providing a normal living conditions for a few wise people for their useful creativity.

What should be done in life at first? What should be done then? Whether it is necessary to build a construction for entertainments or to connect water, electricity and gas to the house of workers? What about house and dwelling for a young family? Where to give birth and bring up children? How to support aged, helpless parents who gave all their energy, forces and means for the family?

The real life shows sequence of specific actions in a simple and available way. **At first it is necessary to satisfy vital needs of all citizens. Only after that it is possible to build entertaining constructions. IF A PERSON IS HUNGRY AND NAKED THEN DANCING AND FOOTBALL ARE NOT NECESSARY TO HIM!**

To stop the wildness and thoughtlessness, it is effective and useful to provide the public word to the Reasonable Thinker with analytical mind and rare combination of high personal qualities: depths of logical thinking "below a sea bottom" (abilities to see not only plants and bottom in the water, but also roots of plants in bottom), abilities to provide proofs which nobody will be able to refute, the independence of opinions without pleasing to someone, courage before possible negative reaction of other people, absence of desire to be enriched at the expense of other people and unindifference to bad living conditions of poor people, etc. As a rule, the recollection of wise advice at the right time of life limits the manifestation of the "ugly", wild, bad actions.

The bitter Truth of life shows that many modest great thinkers remained unnoticed and unrecognized during their lifetime because of blind indifference of surrounding people! That is such a sad story.

Realization of the intellectual capacity and physical abilities

In the process of accumulation of valuable life experience a person can develop the ability to express his thoughts in accurate, distinct, clear and understandable way. If this ability is combined with deep intensive thinking "to the bottom of truth lake" without narrow knowledge of concrete specialty and traditions of local residents then such a person has an opportunity to say a wise thought in the form of Truth. It is interesting that wise saying of a stranger in other state admires and leads to recognition of a useful contribution to human existence. A similar saying of the companion, of person whom you know causes the dismissive statement: "I know it without your help!". In this case the wise thought unfairly falls into oblivion.

THE CREATIVITY can be true and false. The true creativity is always created by really talented person by heavy, long and tiresome work. Works for ages in fine, perfective aspects are the result of such creativity. Normal people feel a good surprise, admiration and gratitude to the creator of the magnificent architectural work, tremendous grandiose painting and construction for useful practical use by many people.

Life continues under different conditions, the originality of which can make a substantial adjustment into human actions. For example, a person suddenly begins to do things that are not given by Mother-Nature. This incomprehensible fact is especially expressed in Pseudo-actors, Pseudo-musicians and Modernists of Art. There is no charisma and diligence but there is a strong wish to be a great artist, singer and musician! Thus, the various "modernists" appear.

The true high Art is possible only in the presence of natural feeling of proportions of product shape, combinations of colours and harmony of sounds, etc. When there are no such abilities, it is necessary to play a role of Original-Modernist. If such a person cannot get an elegant combination of smooth, natural transitions of sounds on a musical instrument, then it is possible without any logic, to influence roughly by sharp "sounds" on mentality of the listener. And such "untalented person" can speak to the general public as the "Modern Modernist" as founder of the new direction of musical art! How about the false "artists"?

The true beauty of the image requires from artist's nature the existence of combination of ability to see, feel the world around in hardly noticeable details and interconnection of elements of object of attention. For example, the Great Leonardo da Vinci was not lazy he walked around the city, watched interesting, original appearance of individuals and sketched especially interesting details of the Person: fingers, facial expression, layout of each hair on the head of the old man, etc. It took a lot of time and effort. The ingenious Artist considered that it is normal and natural to toil many years of life on a piece of art.

What is the use to toil, when you can quickly, without observance of laws of the Nature, carelessly to dub canvas with a brush? Assignment to such lazy modernist a rank of the Artist and, even, "the Great Modernist Artist" amaze the normal person! Those who admit them do not understand that thereby they show the personal naturally incompetence and humiliate really Great artists from God.

ERUDITION in any field of activity is valuable aesthetic quality of the well-mannered person. It allows you to fantasize endlessly and find the Optimum when solving the problem.

Creative Personalities

It is accepted to speak about the man "with a capital letter M" and outstanding abilities with deep respect: "The person is Blacksmith, Mechanic, Designer, Cook, Violinist, Artist from God, Exciting Haydn, Sunny Vivaldi, Awesome Mozart, Powerful Bach from God".

Outstanding abilities and talents of individuals reveal in each field of activity. These people devote their life to manifestation and realization of the ability to create something that surrounding people with undisclosed abilities cannot. The creative person goes deep into the "native" field of activity despite negative reaction, or rather indifference of surrounding people. He does not want to waste time for something else. However, the reality forces to earn money for food, clothes, etc. This time of life **steals time for creativity. The Talent does not manage to create a lot of things as a gift to all people.** It is sad to state this. It is a pity that surrounding people do not wish to understand this.

There is one reason of this phenomenon: every person considers himself as a talented, outstanding and even the genius! He cannot and does not want even to imagine that there are people above the level of his ability to create something outstanding. Therefore, he "shuts his eyes" and completely ignore the superiority of the colleague. Especially this thoughtlessness is inherent to "chiefs". As a result society loses very valuable in every respect spiritual and material capitals. Many people unreasonably prevent filling of the "common moneybox" by physical resources and original, effective, useful ideas. At best, people imperceptibly, secretly use free fruits of work of silent modest Talent.

In reality of life in ancient times all magnates wished to have the magnificent palaces and churches to expand their popularity. Therefore they involuntarily used abilities of ingenious people and created good conditions for their creativity. Castles, palaces, churches were always filled with works of great sculptors, artists and engineers. Therefore the positive factor of development of humanity is a fair recognition of a high contribution of magnates in creation of high culture in architecture and aesthetics.

It is interesting to remember bright historical actions and the facts of creativity of talented and ingenious people of Humankind.

Pericles (the V century BC) – the Great statesman of Ancient Greece, the speaker with clear mind and rare natural gift – sense of proportion and beauty, organized government rationally and reasonably. He introduced public duties for magnates: benevolent distribution of material benefits and money to poor citizens, execution of the state positions at their own expense, etc. Pericles devoted a HALF of the income of the state fund for education, upbringing and culture of life of all citizens. Pericles support of creation of material and ethic conditions for creativity of great ingenious artists, sculptors and architects allowed them to build magnificent palaces in Athens in short term and turn the capital of Greece with rural image into the Example of Beauty with world authority, into the Example of Perfection of the Maker's Personality.

Parthenon (Temple of Athena) was built by ingenious architects Callicrates and Ictinus, the Goddess Athena Parthenos was created by the sculptor and architect Phidias, the Discobolus – the young man in movement, was made by sculptor Myron, the theorist of art Polykleitos developed laws of harmony and proportionality of person's parts in a perfect image of Doryphoros, etc. Each of authors of these ideals of Perfection of human forms and proportions and architectural constructions is the pride of the Golden Age of Greece.

The historian Plutarch appraised these architectural monuments of a classical era clearly: "Each of these works of art was so fine that made the impression of something worthwhile from time immemorial, thanks to their cheerfulness they are still seem something young and just arisen".

Why the modernity cannot give birth to the ruler of the state similar to Pericles to organize Balance: "Rich man + People"? After all, there is the **example to follow**! There is a wish to live and create near the Great Godsends!

The young Alexander of Macedon (the IV century BC) offered to the poor wise Diogenes all conditions for more effective manifestation of mind to the benefit of all people. However, Diogenes's specific nature did not wish to use these and he continued to sleep in a barrel and give help in the form of wise good advice in the course of conversation for everyone. For this reason, we cannot enjoy his wisdom now.

We know the reasonable and useful for people actions of sane rich people in the Roman Empire of the first century BC. For example, Agrippa, the associate of the ruler Augustus, after receiving of unlimited capital, constructed the water supply for all inhabitants of Rome (not only for himself), temple the Pantheon, etc. Agrippa did not begin only accumulate and store the capital he spent it for the benefit of all people. These constructions have been bringing benefit to people for 2000 years!

Reasonable personality of Gaius from the rich Cilnius family known as the Maecenas has been the sample of extremely useful and rational attitude to the people for full manifestation of their outstanding talents in the maximum extent possible, for 2000 years. Why the Maecenas could easily, freely and rationally accept natural benevolent actions? Obviously, he made for himself a simple conclusion: if the child, teenager or young man has a talent for Creativity, it is NECESSARY PROMPTLY to create the optimum conditions for his development and manifestation! Really, the earlier the Talent, the Genius will stop thinking and wasting time, forces, and health for production of food, clothes and housing, the more time will be given for creativity useful for all people. The works of Geniuses do not have term restrictions of influence on the person, they are eternal! That's why the Maecenas, for example, presented the estates for full creativity to such Talents of Poetry as: Vergil ("Aeneid"), Horace (Odes, Satires), Ovid (Love Elegies and Councils for lovers).

The king of France Francis I (the XVI century AD) provided to the full disposal to great Leonardo da Vinci the beautiful castle with the service personnel for full freedom of creativity of the Genius of Humanity.

In the following centuries the rare cases of financial support even to the famous, pronounced, glorified Art Geniuses are little known to people. On the contrary, all property and pictures were confiscated because of debts from Rembrandt (the XVII century AD) the author of cheerful art of the Netherlands with innovative approach to classical plots. After this he lived in poverty for the last 13 years of life. The Matchless Antonio Vivaldi, the author of refreshing music which forces the soul to rise into the sky, and the body to slide in dance without any efforts, died in the first half of the XVIII century AD, forgotten and sick. The Great Mozart died in poverty at the end of the XVIII century AD at the age of 35. There was no money for his funeral, so he was buried in a common grave for homeless people, location of which is not known up to now. How many works of the highest art the mankind did not inherit because of reduction of lifetime of Geniuses due to the fault of mediocre people?

And still, the Great personalities got deserved recognition of descendants and immortality by their unequalled creativity, despite the primitive actions of intellectually and ethically limited people.

When the THINKER is ahead of time, the short-sighted situation turns out: his thoughts and creativity are not necessary to contemporaries! So they live in poverty as "cranks", "dreamers" and "otherworldly" people. There are pleasant exceptions, for example: Leonardo da Vinci, Lomonosov, etc.

Certainly, real life is capable to promulgate recognition of outstanding abilities at certain people. It is not always possible to hide or ignore the obviously expressed outstanding Talent or Genius at the modest personality in forcible or indifferent way. The person with elevated mind will not stoop to megalomania. Therefore he wishes to waste time only for reflections, analysis and development of strategy of problem solving. Naturally, he will be glad to appearance of individuals who expressed the desire to realize his innovative idea, and will be disappointed if it will be ignored and denied. However, nature will force to continue the development of new ideas that arise automatically in the head with new circumstances of life. The brain of the Talent and the Genius cannot function in a different way.

The WISE HERMIT in the old days had a significant freedom of actions. He did not need a lot. He only had to support the vital needs of the body and brain and that was enough. Bandits did not rob him because the beggar has nothing to take. The Hermit usually gave to people effective advice how reasonably and usefully solve problems in a hopeless situation.

In modern living conditions it is problematic to the Hermit to be the traveller ("vagabond") or to choose a cave in mountains. The peace officers in the states can immediately require documents, arrest you and insult by mistrust. Curious people will also bother him. Therefore, the "modern hermit" is very limited and relative concept. Nowadays, any retiree can seclude at the summer cottage or in the apartment at the desk and devote the rest of life for creativity and comprehension of the living conditions of people on the Earth.

Ideally the hermit may be accidentally found and properly appreciated by the new Maecenas with high level of Mind and Culture. This will allow the Hermit to receive optimum conditions for effective creativity of new ideas for the benefit of humankind in the fullest possible extent, because life is limited by Destiny.

The real SCIENTIST, PROFESSOR in modern life is the outstanding expert in concrete activity area. His purpose is to think deeply, to develop new ideas, create new technologies for all humankind and to prepare new professional community. It requires time, because the new idea, as a rule, is born at intensive reflection at any time of day. Therefore it would be useful for Humankind to relieve the Thinker from caring about the everyday realities of life.

Recognition of Talent and Genius

Time after time Almighty gifts all people over the Earth with outstanding abilities, throwing on the Earth seeds of Talent and Genius from outer space. Some can get more, some can get less or nothing at all. This seed can fall on any place, on any child with his birth. However it doesn't matter how high their material conditions, the level of their intellect and abilities, politeness, social status is. Which child gets this unique felicity to create and make something eminent? Nobody knows that.

TALENT is an extraordinary high level of man's ability for some kind of an occupation or mental activity. It is a changeless treasure given by the nature to any person. All parents want their child to be gifted. Involuntary they suggest talented person as the one who for sure will have all remaining qualities: an intellect, kindness, performance capability, hard-working, etc. But in reality such a combination is rare to meet as the person with negative moral character can also get Intellect and Talent.

For example a talented joiner, who supplies the court of the Queen of Great Britain with wonderful furniture, was narrow minded. Regard shown by Queen to talented but helpless "bone-head", "fool" speaks of her high moral character: the high level of Intellect, Kindness and Intelligence. Some useful trick appears from this example: it is good to give a possibility for every narrow minded person to recognize his talent using it for his own and people's good. So there is a double use: to turn "a sleazy person" into a useful "hard-worker".

"God's gift" of modern computer technologies practical usage impresses us especially. Genius child can quickly and easily understand, learn and use them with no experience. For example he can he even crack incredibly complicated program for protection of data privacy of some bank or financial institution, drawn up by skilled and educated specialists.

In real life there is one unanswered question in normal man's behaviour: "When is it viable to recognize Talent and

Genius officially? The most wide-spread habit is to admit only manager, chief or headman's primary, high personal qualities. However all stripes manager's way of thinking comes into effect: If I'm a manager all the rest are subordinate. They are less smart than me and nobody can exceed me in mental and creative activity!" There is a short adage saying: "I'm the boss, you're the butt. You are in charge and I'm nobody." According to this habit there can only be a silent understanding of the fact that somebody else also has Talent. A natural question appears in this situation: What good may do such a silent behaviour of people around?".

It is clever and useful to show simple goodwill, honour and with open heart to say to the public with joy in their hearts delight Almighty gift to his friend, or companion, and to assist in the implementation of its innovations for the benefit of all people. For example when you listen to Vivaldi you are admired by The Talent of Mankind, you feel your soul calming, you breathe gets deeper and you want to fly high into the sky, enjoying the fact that you live, you are not stuck in the darkness, chained into daily routine.

The GENIUS has an unconventional Global Thinking. Results of his work belong to the Mankind (not to only one country). There is an old saying: "Everything is simple, but of genius!"

So why don't people notice the Genius of Simplicity within his lifetime? Why should he live in bad conditions spending a bulk of his time in search of simple means of living instead of working for the good of Mankind? Nevertheless his felicities are spread before the eyes! But his behaviour is completely different; he has a habit to do things which an ordinary people consider to be absurd and useless. He can be Good at thinking, art, but Helpless in real life situations. There are enough reasons to give him a dig or to joke. That's why recognition and appreciation of the Genius within his lifetime is a rare exception! A lot of rich people, feeling an overindulgence can't even imagine that somebody can be smarter. So they can easily humble The Genius and even starve him from simple means of living.

The Genius of Simplicity doesn't make money by all means, acting nonmoral, neglecting other people's needs. He can't be fierce and immoral. For example Saint Francis the Great after his beatific vision gave all his staff (property) to poor people and was earning money only on feeding. But he did not turn into a drone. He was working hard at the church building at any weather and then became a Preacher of Good Man's Traits. After his death some clever priests found the God's Gift in his actions and sainted him!

In general Leaders knowingly did not let The Inherent Genius become famous. But thoughts of these people are not at stop. Upon their hook Men of Genius always offered simple solutions of any difficult problems in people's life. In consequence of evident practical use of these ideas some of thinkers unknowingly became well-known personalities. They got famous and made the History of Mankind.

Manifestation of Breeding

THE TRUTH OF LIFE can be sweet and bitter. Nobody wants even to hear the bitter truth and try to make a useful output for himself. Although, in practice, there is a known form of «male talk ", which allows quietly listen to this truth, to think and to correct their behaviour, realize efficiencies. Violence is always unpleasant experience. However, is it possible to live in a society of people without limit of harmful actions and behaviour? Forced useful violence is necessary primarily for families, children, elderly people, for those who are mentally and physically weak, helpless people. In the scale of the state it's necessary to limit freedom of harmful manifestations, wild, terrible acts by individuals to the detriment of all citizens.

It is pleasant to see, to feel DECENT behaviour of the citizen. Honourable man, even in his thought cannot wish anything bad to another person. He has the natural qualities to help other people voluntarily with personal pleasure and with elegant manners.

In past centuries, **True Upbringing** was inherent to aristocrats. They could not leave the house in ugly, outdated clothes, being unshaved, unkempt. Their moves were accurate, correct and beautiful. Greetings to lady a man always presented gracefully with undisguised delight.

False, fictitious, only the visible manners shown, as a rule, by people from ordinary families, who did not have an opportunity to get proper education and upbringing. After growing up and coming to wealth and power these people started to copy aristocratic manners of bygone years, since the XIX century AD. At the beginning of the XXI century BC there was a sharp decline in the education of citizens in so-called ' civilized ' countries.

For example, a modern famous performance director, had having productive relationships with mannered performing artists, suddenly came to the official festival in a trendy, expensive jacket and torn jeans! A lot of people present there applauded to incredible originality of the director! And it is instead of turning away from indecent, wild celebrity's outfit, showing their true contempt of unfailing respect for the basic rules of life of well -mannered person. Thus, he showed his true natural essence! It turns out that he was only a visible Intellectual, not true.

Similar problems exist in the modern world for people who grew up in the wild atmosphere of streets in an environment where satisfaction of animal needs and instincts, disregard

116

of the people around, selfishness in its full force dominates.

A **boor** in most cases is uniquely characterized by his appearance. His unkempt face, messed up hair,' Undressing ' look in his eyes, constantly open mouth, loose lips, stubbleness, ill-fitting and casually arranged clothes, vulgar manners in his moves, frivolous jokes, ETC can be seen afar.

Here is a simple example of the lack of 'care about your neighbour.' Man walks down the road and sees a strong wind tumbled large tree branches. Indifferent person will pass by, the other will only swear. A normal person will quietly remove a branch from the road for women, children, elderly people, transport could easily walk.

Here is one more example. Very often, people, not thinking kindly, throw bottles, bags, candy labels anywhere in the city and in the countryside. Such wild attitude to the environment surprises normal man's psyche. So, by this 'little nothing of life' the level of moral behaviour can be simply and reliably determined. And as for all people (and for rude also) it is pleasant to see clean houses, streets, lively mother-nature. Therefore, it is a time to return to the practice of useful comments aloud about the **inadmissibility** of ugly deeds of uneducated people! It **should not be** guided by a wild, immoral concept of the motto "**Freedom is permissiveness** "!

Available for all modern higher education also contributes to the formation of false politeness. Atmosphere of the university unwittingly makes a lot of students desire to imitate manners of their educated teachers. In this process, people with natural friendly qualities, deeply and quickly gets true education of pleasant communicational manners. But man with wild natural qualities gets only visible breeding. In the time of offences and material losses he immediately shows his true face in rough, angry, contemptuous, insolent reactive actions.

History shows that even some of the heirs of monarchs, state governors, having received a highly moral education, after coming to power suddenly changed their moral life benchmarks. For example, the great philosopher Seneca (I century AD) adequately trained Nero, who successfully put into practice the criteria of high morality during first years. And then permissiveness of authorities has revived Nero's negative nature of essence and it turned into a villain.

Culture of People's Mutual Relations

Cultural behaviour is always pleasant for people around. How wonderful is it to have a sense of beauty, harmony of reality, to feel the charm of graceful manners, refinement of the taste, mesmerizing rhetoric! Man's elegant, expressive hand, body, legs, head movements are especially attractive. That's all about the way he sits at the table, in what position, how he rises, walks, talks, laughs, looks at somebody and something, ETC. Most people's eyes are the mirror of the soul, of spiritual essence. By their expression we can determine the level of intellect and moral nature of the person, his character, level of education and manifestations of sincerity. In addition, eyes can determine possible future and destiny. An oscillation beautiful leaves on the trees and movements of lions, swans; ETC can clearly serve as analogue of human behaviour

How useful it is for boys and girls to pay a due attention to learning higher values of life of an educated person! Realizing the concept of Culture, young people are guaranteed to enjoy an interesting and eventful life. Even in far future they will remind about this knowledge with great satisfaction, pride, awareness of importance of past times. And get used to observing high ethical standards (ethica - lat.) of moral behaviour civilized man is quite easy!

How pleasant it is when you forget some of things at the entrance to the institution at the store, then you come back and find everything in its place intact. Immediately you get a feeling of soul comfort, pleasant awareness of respect for all people around! These soul radiations certainly approach all the people who saw your thing and did not take it. Later these people unconsciously get surprised with lifting mood, luck in business. There is a benefit for lots of people! So, as we still do not know a lot of laws of nature, we do not realize that we all live in the world of the intangible waves with invisible structure.

Cultural, educated, well-mannered person is able to subtly state his thoughts and express them gracefully to the public. Such a demonstration of his nature can also properly assess in his brain brilliant thoughts of the others and react accordingly. In practice, during conversation it is useful exercise patience: first silently listen to your interlocutor, witnesses of the event, learn all the circumstances and then express your opinion.

The Appearance of a Citizen

Appearance of a citizen points out at his level of breeding. At the beginning of the XXI th century permissiveness under the name of "freedom of life" reached the complete degradation of the appearance of many people in civilized countries quite naturally. To draw attention to themselves at any price, they followed the example of homeless people unreasonably. Nobody is surprised at seeing known, famous, popular people in the image of homeless persons on the scene, on TV, during the holidays: untidy, unshaved, unkempt with sticking tufts of hair, in torn jeans The limit of the modern degradation of the high ethics in relations is a "street" type of a conductor's clothes from the classical symphonic orchestra and the same of a soloist.

119

Such a disregard towards high cultural values testifies to the absence of modesty and loss of decency and shame in the real essence of a person.

Cultural Level

A citizen's, scientist's, state official's NAME with a high reputation can't be bought. A NAME can be acquired only after a proper evaluation and recognition of a person's remarkable merits by his colleagues and people around.

The history of development of mankind formed an ideal to be followed in the process of cognition of rules of civilization of the human society.

A **cultivated person** has a rich soul, sympathy, unselfishness, can control his own high ethic behaviour, and understands what is useful and harmful for the surrounding world (*). His goodwill, his feeling of own dignity, his wish to do noble deeds, independence of his judgments on the base of justice excludes any violence – all this is always willingly accepted by surrounding people.

Personal natural qualities for sure give the notion "Cultivated Person" interesting peculiarities. For example, a personality with no high level of natural qualities always observes civilized rules of relations of citizens in any situation in life as a result of reasonable education. That's why he can be called **"an Educated Cultivated Person."**

Non persistent from nature personalities incline to self-removal from the wish to achieve a goal working hard. Such cultivated personalities can reconcile to personal loss for the sake of peace of mind. They can be characterized as **"Mild Cultivated Persons."**

Vice versa, there are personalities with strong characters who want to achieve their goals spending much time during life, working hard and doing deeds firmly. In this situation one can speak of "**a Hard Cultivated Person.**"

If an educated person has inherent ability to think deeply and to see far, has a higher training and a fundamental volume of knowledge, ETC, a very interesting combination of different notions such as high intellect, knowledge, useful education of ethic forms of behaviour can be formed. In this way the highest, ideal type is formed known as "**an Intellectual Cultivated Person.**"

A personality with great life experience, having a high level of knowledge of natural laws and those of people's life, used to a constant process of spontaneous reflection for the benefit of mankind, having high level of morality from mother-nature, can be called "**a Wise Cultivated Person.**"

Real life ascertains a notion "**False Cultivated Person**" because a citizen with low natural moral qualities can show an uncivilized reaction in a difficult life situation. Besides, a former external civilized cultural behaviour disappears.

(*) Choogin V.V. and Chepelyuk E.V., "INTELLIGENTIS"< Way to perfection. Pub. KHNTU, Kherson, Ukraine, 2008, pp 80, ISBN 978-966-2207-01-9. In Russian.

CHAPTER 4

Principal Peculiarities of Organization and Effective Functioning of a Reasonable, Just, Uniform Country "Earth"

Following the analysis of people's real-time being carried out in the previous chapters, let's consider a possible way to the Uniform Country "EARTH".

At the present time there are states in the world, that were formed on the base of different lands' union (and conquests in the past years) where people of different nationalities and beliefs live. From time to time this circumstance leads to conflicts with the usage of force on the part of the ruling nationality.

The task of clever, far-seeing, honest people is to show a wise **awareness of the necessity to organize** a Reasonable,

Just Society "EARTH." To do this, it is necessary to organize a wise education of posterity fulfilling only one condition: execution of people's power must be given to energetic, cheerful, honest, wise people! Aren't there such 50÷100÷1000 people in the states with the population of 1÷10÷50 million? The problem (ostensibly) is in a real search of people of high morality. Why do PEOPLE (overwhelming majority of citizens) show a negative agreement to limitation of their rights and choose (supposedly) energetic, amoral, unworthy people with megalomania to political office? This negative phenomenon surprises reasonable, honest people. Its hushing up also surprises these people.

It's high time to stop living unreasonably with mind's restrictions by the previous defective conditions of people's communication between the rich and the poor, between the clever and the stupid, with the contradictions between nations and states. It is high time to begin the process OF SAVING MANKIND by MEANS of SEEING THINGS CLEARLY and of NECESSITY AWARENESS of realizing the first REASONABLE steps into a useful and pleasant FUTURE.

In order to do this it **is necessary to change radically THE RULES of man's living in the whole world SIMULTANIUSLY.** This act seems to be unreal, but desirable, useful because high morality is the BASIS of a normal life. It is sad to say about the reality: without any WISH to govern life in a reasonable direction one can get nothing. That's why children's EDUCATION should be performed by people with high natural qualities, by well-intended, honest, decent, hard-working, modest people with no superiority complex.

Rational Grounds of man's Everyday Life

At the beginning of the analysis of real being conditions it is necessary to realize natural physiological and psychological needs of a human organism and his ability to evaluate reasonably situations of everyday life taking into consideration age, natural qualities and level of education.

An ordinary family man in any state solves ordinary pressing problems: how to provide the family with a normal dwelling, how to feed and provide clothing for the members of the family, how to give children a good education. All the rest is of minor importance, on the background of life. After hard, intensive labour and overstrain, a human organism needs relaxation of muscles and brain. How to put one's mind at ease after a nervous break-down, physical pain, worries, external pressure and stress? To do it, after all the Negative it is useful to come to a pleasant deed and to immerse into the sphere of moral satisfaction with no harm to surrounding people. When pleasant emotions come, there also comes a wish to fly like a bird, to go dancing, running, or to walk in the wood, etc.

It is useful to understand everyday reality: **reasonable conditions of everyday life restrict the appearance** of some natural momentary negative wishes of people. This awareness allows defining a rational style of living of Mankind.

Each person has an individual nature, a measure of understanding and awareness of current circumstances. It is impossible to require an identical understanding of a certain situation of other people. It is reasonable to be resigned to the fact that another person has his or her own opinion and way of thinking. One should never be angry or swear, it is unreasonable. It is useful to contradict your companion with your arguments and look for a compromise (if it helps to solve the problem) or "step aside" silently. If you see negative consequences of the solution proposed by your companion, speak out your rational opinion or judgment firmly without raising your voice and without using unattractive words.

In a family life everyone knows another person's nature. That's why it is easy and better not to provoke a negative reaction of a spouse. It is better to make your personality keep silence and observe peace even though you don't like it. It will bring peace into the family.

Reasonable Consumption of the Products of Vital Activity

Focusing on the necessary level of rational consumption of life comforts is the base of just distribution of revenues and finances between people without fantastic satisfaction of specific wishes of oligarchs (when hungry and poor people are available).

Minimum requirements of all people MUST be satisfied in the whole world totally. Medical workers can define natural limits of quantity and volume of all useful kinds of provision for people of any build, sphere of activity and age.

During all the period of work it is useful to deduct into the **Pension Saving Fund** regularly and willingly any sum of money to provide normal conditions of living in the old age after the natural loss of physical and mental abilities. It is useful for successful businessmen in the sphere of large-scale and ultra-large-scale business to make allocations to the **Guaranteed Pension Fund** to provide a minimal necessary level of life for all the old people in a mini-state.

It is high time for rich people on the planet to understand the simple truth: each person's **nature**, any living being's nature has **a limit of quantity** in consuming goods of life, for example, food. Having an enormous capital, nobody can eat two loaves of bread, a kilo of butter, a whole sheep, five watermelons, two kilos of apples or drink a bucket of juice at one time, etc. Is it also possible to use ten jackets, coats, cars at one time? Why is it necessary to buy an island visited by an oligarch only some days a year? And so on and so forth. **Why is it necessary to long to have endless quantities of life comforts without a possibility of their rational use?** Where is here an elementary sound sense of actions? Think and stop!

Man's Labour

First, you have to understand and realize: to whom, for what and how fairly to pay for the labour for the good of all citizens and families.

In ancient times, the most powerful person voluntarily committed the hardest and heaviest action for the benefit of his family and tribe, so he had to eat more than others. Then the most powerful man usurped the functions of the Governor, Lord and began ordering his brothers and relatives where and how to work. To maintain his person and the soldiers, freed from daily work, the Governor introduced a Collection of tribute and taxes. After the appearance of priests in the life of society, an excuse to raise taxes on ordinary working people reappeared.

Everyone knows and understands that a peasant works on land from dawn to dusk, from spring to winter, and a landlord embezzles most of the profits from the sale of his crop. Blacksmith working in difficult conditions, producing tools and means of labour, earns for the family a shameful minimum. Weavers, sewers, fishermen, etc. work just as hard.

So, gradually, the difference in paying for serious hard labour of **an ordinary citizen** and visible "work" of '**owners**' increased repeatedly, under various pretexts. This unjust, inhumane ratio wage survived up to the present time.

Rapid technological progress in the XX century, especially in the field of computer science, has led to extensive degradation of the existing system of wealth distribution in the world. This statement seems unreasonable, but works only at the first glance.

Today most of young people for some reason do not want to work physically. It is much more pleasant and preferable for them to stay in a warm room by the computer. Who's going to grow grains, vegetables, fruits, work with metal, produce fabric, sew clothes, put up buildings, etc.?

To give a reasonable estimation of Just system of remuneration it is advizable to analyze the main types of human labour first.

Manual Labour

Labour of **peasants** on the land is dedicated to tillage, planting, water irrigation, cleaning of weeds, shoots' gartering, harvesting, etc. Here **we cannot do without manual labour!** At old times all the harvest was carried out by hands only! While doing so ALL the fruits were collected in good condition and undamaged. That's why they were kept for a long period of consumption (during autumn, winter, spring) without using any chemicals. With the invention and development of technology the process of reducing the cost of a peasants' labour and harvesting got underway. However, mechanized harvesting (the result of long term work) led to unreasonable damage and devastation of a significant amount of fruit.

For example, earlier the cotton was plucked from the bush and put into a bag by hands. Now mechanisms suck fibre shrubs together with leaves and bark ("garbage"). Now a necessity to create ginneries appeared. Textile companies began to receive damaged and shortened fibre in entangled condition. That's the length of intact fibres which determines the level of cotton quality and the possibility to create thin filaments for excellent smooth fabrics! Wastes on the textile enterprises increased substantially. As a result, the same piece of land began to provide people with less fibre in a normal state of nature, and the number of vacancies declined significantly. However, modern businessmen do not care about this fact!

Next. Vegetables, fruits from trees, etc. began to be collected by machines. For tomatoes not to bruise, farming specialists invented dense, but tasteless breeds. Apples started to be collected by the tree vibration, so the damage of the fruit while falling became inevitable. Nowadays, only on a small plot of land in the country, people (mostly retired) can observe the tradition of compliance of reasonable rules to harvest soft fruits of all kinds: **"You pick one delicate pear tomato, a bunch of grapes, apple and put it neatly into the cart or box"**. It eliminates the possibility of the of 20 ÷ 30 % crop's death!

Children of wildlife rip off and eat the grass and leaves only in the amount necessary for their organism! But, the most intelligent beings - people - **deliberately destroy vain fruits of nature and peasant labour** by modern mechanized methods of harvesting. Thus, irrational modern tradition of mechanized harvesting **of easily damaged fruit is the demonstration of overt crimes against Nature and Man!**

Of course, it is possible to continue using mechanized harvesting of relatively solid, dense fruit plants in a protective shell, such as wheat, rye, etc.

Not everyone is able to withstand the hard labour of Peasant. However, mankind cannot do without it, because everyone needs a full and delicious feeding without chemicals dangerous for people.

So who should have tangible benefits to a greater extent? Manufacturer or speculator? Workaholic peasant works in any weather on earth - mother, and buyer- dealers for little price take harvest and sell it to 2 ÷ 3 times (and 10 times) more expensive! No smell of Justice under this action felt!

Labour of the working class is not easier. In addition, the worker has to work in often hazardous conditions: for example, in steel mills, in metal smelting, in deep coal mines, chemical plants, moving cargo by ship and aircraft, etc.

Mental Labour

To make something of steal, wood, chemical materials you should **invent** a product design **first**, then create an experimental sample, test it, remedy deficiencies and test it again. All these operations demand using laborious Inherent Talents. Combination of thinking abilities and smart professional hand managing is the basis of the material oeuvre art with the largest possible outcome.

As the result, working equipment, necessary for mankind, can be made by people who have just one of these inherent gifts. If these two eminent abilities are harmonized in one person, the birth of more time proof, effective and useful working equipment is possible.

Before production of any tool this standard procedure must be undertaken:

- execute an examination of reality
- analyze the problem
- give a birth to idea
- find the tactics of its materialization
- find materials and working equipment
- accommodate well disposed working conditions
- produce an experimental sample
- test the sample

- produce several variants of new goods and test them in real conditions

- publicize and start industrial input of new goods.

So some sad question appears here again: "Why do inventors of useful working equipment very often stay in shadow? They spend bulk of their lives trying to get vital means of live for their family instead of creative work for the good of Mankind". In such a way we cramp, prohibit, keep under an effective progression forward to more advanced, smart and pleasant living. The reason is quite clear: it is hidden in undesired demonstration of our narrow thinking. To tell more exact it is in our thoughtlessness.

Specialist's Labour

An engineer organizes and manages the work of employees on the factory, works out new hardware design, machinery, technologies, carries out researches, etc. For effective work he demands full technical education to be able to make practical use of the main laws of mathematics, physics, chemistry, cybernetics, etc.

Medical workers have distinct, strongly-marked labour characteristics for the good of man's health. There is a small number of people who can cut man's body, set a bone, live through the death of a patient, etc. without making one's blood creep. Surgeon who has both knowledge and skill of careful, delicate and decisive usage of the scalpel is a rare treasure of mankind. Physician, able to feel, see and notice signs of deterioration of internal organs and body parts is also an invaluable treasure! Practically it takes a long time for these Talents to appear as it is necessary to get and to bring up to date practical skills of everyday hard-working. Those who protect our health: doctors, nurses, pharmacists, teachers have some defined features of their nature: they are Philanthropic and Patient. Not everyone has got it! As medical workers provide us with things we need the most (Health and Feeling of well-being), people all over the world should agree to give worth payment for their work.

A real, true Historian should have a well-developed feeling of Farseeing based on The Power of Thinking. In reality anyone who will take the trouble can write "historical memorials". It is enough for them just to have a superiority complex of their narrow mind. They are these false historians who always distort the truth in order to please The Leaders of the country and because of the nationalism based on preconceived selection of the facts, which corresponds their philosophy. People think that the history is written truly, argumentatively. But in reality "It" is a disguised Lie! Except for such pseudo- historians, some writers can also distort the history.

It is difficult to find **The Real Historian,** a person able to show true logic of events which occurred during the past ages objectively, with no interest, not being affected by the current life conditions. In reality readers, students, statesmen don't know whom to believe! So there is the only one thing left: the reader himself should have a look at all present facts (available for him) paying no attention to opinions of "experts" and "historians". Only "cold truth" doesn't distort the history, which allows a person to get own vision of historical events.

Presence of practically **immense** amount of historical facts, placed in libraries of different countries worldwide is an objective factor. That's why it is advizable to analyze only specific facts. Among them are peace and war-time conditions, cultural values, progress and regress of existence, etc. Theoretically it is helpful to consider each side of men's life by certain Genius possessing strongly pointer streak in certain sphere of life for further comparison with the results of historical researches. On the ground of these writings an Analyst will be able to state the logic of historical events of Mankind most closely resembling to the truth.

A pedagogue, a teacher, tutor, kindergartner determine the conditions of foundation of each person's life productivity and further soul harmony. To make an effective use of this process a real, true **"Teacher+ Kindergartner"** should be able to control his emotions and to recognize, to identify inborn aptitude for 'gentle' effecting child's psychoactivity without any visible compulsion. Professional education, high-toned internal qualities of nature, aesthetic look help The Teacher to be a role model.

One more important factor: The Teacher must use the procedure of student's **ACADEMIC PERFORMANCE RATING AS THE FINAL STEP OF EDUCATIONAL PROSCESS,** BRAIN BUILDING, TRAINING OF THINKING, because today abstract written examination has just a formal status and it seems to be independent of personal traits of the Teacher.

Fair System of Remuneration

For ages, the system of remuneration has existed as a variety of symbols. At the beginning of trade between the citizens of the primitive state formations there were pieces of beautiful stones, gold, silver used. Then people contrived coins. After inventing printing on paper, symbols of value started to be used in the form of "money". Each state still prints special images on paper notes. Therefore, settlements between citizens and public authorities in different countries are quite hindered.

Man's greed and profit chase constantly lead to money devaluation. As a result, the situation often turns unreasonable: production cost of banknotes becomes higher than its face-value. New specimens of banknotes have to be invented, spending on it money of ordinary working people. With development of technology, cashless payments by electronic cards came to be used. However, cards will never replace cash banknotes and coins in "real" everyday life when paying, for example, on the street for ice cream, flowers, tea and coffee, etc. In addition, international cooperation, tourism, relocation of people to more developed countries causes high expenditures on currency exchange. This waste of money is provided by many normal people, who turn into non-productive "parasites".

During the period of construction of the Indivisible Country of "Earth", it is reasonable to start the official move to a **uniform system of cash settlements**. It shouldn't devaluate through the years of use.

On what is it rational to spend money first of all, on entertainment or on arrangement elementary necessary conditions of human existence and development of creativity for the good of all mankind?

A majority of working people have a lot of free time after work or on weekends. Therefore, it is useful to go out together voluntarily on Saturday or Sunday and clean up surrounding space around the house, in the park, on the street, to help the helpless elderly people. What a great pleasure for your Soul to see that your unselfish work is useful, to see smiles of people around and to please those people, for whom IT was intended! This is the good for all people, especially for younger generation. That's how we ARE SUPPOSED TO LIVE IN A PLEASANT AURA, CREATED BY BENEVOLENCE! Unfortunately, in modern life free volunteer work is carried out mostly by elderly people, retirees. The only reminder to all of workers is that the amount of pension should provide fair satisfaction of minimally essential needs of life.

WHO HAVE TO BE PAID MORE? The answer is simple: the one who brings the greatest benefit to the people! It's fair to consider, that material goods distribution is proportional to invested toil on the welfare for the all of working people.

For example, not everyone (especially male) is able to work in kindergarten, because kindergartners feed babies, wash bums, withstand whims, crying, screaming and educate in a child mental and physical fundamentals of life, ethics of friendly relations and lay the foundation of a beautiful and useful life. While teacher's salary in today's kindergarten is the lowest! It is an example of saying: "Everything is upside down!"

In the old days Ruler received more goods, than Servant. In a real national state People is the Ruler, i.e. the working people, the producers of physical and intellectual product. All "public servants" are people's Servants. Exactly from this accordance it is necessary to start with a reasonable definition of the remuneration level.

Practically, **a statesman's salary must not exceed the minimum wage of a working citizen.** This ratio will guarantee People's Servant natural desire to improve living conditions of the citizens. Moreover, it eliminates the negative desire of rising to power those people, who thirst for excessive enrichment at the expenses of simple citizens.

The highest level of goods distribution should be provided to intelligent individuals, who make benefit for ALL mankind. Among them are developers of new ideas, innovative technologies and technological solutions for the manufacturing of real products for the benefit of all people on the Earth.

The second highest level of goods distribution should belong to producers of spiritual values and material products.

It is fair to provide **the third level** of goods distribution to "People's Servants" such as public figures, government officials, economists, bankers, merchants, entertainers, etc.

Highly qualified specialist's salary should be calculated within reasonable limits, depending on the working capital or profit of a particular enterprise, producing and selling of a specific product.

SLUGGARDS, producing neither material nor spiritual goods, mustn't be paid with the state salary on behalf of the nation. For example, it is high time to stop the imprisonment of criminals at the expenses of the budget of ordinary working citizens. Nowadays a potential criminal calmly prepares to commit a wrongful action. He is confident, that lawyer can protect him, that he can sit idly and serve time in prison free of charge. But at the same time the victim of his attack should pay for the treatment of obtained injuries from family budget or be buried at the expense of their relatives. We came to see that diabolic inequality between Victim's rights and offender's rights is legalized! Who should have more rights? Supposedly **"smart" modern jurisprudence in all countries all over the world actually provides THE LEADERSHIP OF CRIMINALS' LAWS!!** It is the obvious disrespect of human dignity, the distortion of notion "Justice"!

Let the criminals do hard work BY THEMSELVES and let THEM maintain a functioning justice system, prison, and guards from the fund of their earnings. The modern worldwide system of quiet, lazy punishment at the expense of the innocent citizens is a clear manifestation of THE UNDISGUISED DISRESPECT FOR normal WORKING PEOPLE!

Taxes

The majority of the world's countries **form the state budget on the basis of absurd, primitive system of taxation.**

On principle, from the reasonable position, due to the fair organization of all productive forces there should be **NO TAXES** in the future country EARTH! This surprising (at first sight) statement can be simply and easily solved in any state.

For example, in real life an ordinary Person ennobles the vacant land, by HIMSELF, voluntary and without any payment from operating public authority, grows the fruits and keeps his family with a crop. **Why on earth should he pay obligatory taxes to the state's fund, which is actually disposed by oligarchs?** On the contrary, it would be fair to help organize family business from the state's fund!

The most obvious **source of the incomes for covering 100% of maintenance costs** and work of all government bodies, material security of health care, education, concordance of all branches of economic activity in the state are the **state's enterprises** of industrial and agricultural production. It is enough for them to work at the highest level using the high technologies and to get the high PROFIT level to cover ALL state's expenses. Therefore destroying of **state's enterprises, transferring the whole industries to private hands is the CRIME towards the People! Why should the Profit be given from the former state's enterprises to individuals?** Why do the people silently allow plundering themselves?

Only up **to the BEGINNING of the concrete organization of the Indivisible Country Earth** the procedure of collection taxes has to be used. Thus it is necessary to designate the fair procedure and to take conditions of temporary assignment of taxes, on whom and from whom not to take, from whom it is more and from whom it is less. Let us review the main examples.

The Minimum and Normal income of a family has to provide nature needs of people. For example, every member of the family has the right to consume food from a set of all available products, providing normal operating conditions of an organism with its features. At the same time it is necessary to have the minimum quantity of normal full-fledged clothes for all seasons. There should be enough money for transport, utilities, devices of life, medicine, education, etc.

In real life for the organization of family and small business not even a dime is taken from the state's budget! Citizens voluntary organize the business at their own expense (and for debts). If the citizen earned money abroad and sent them to a family for vital expenses, i.e. enriched the state also, why does he have to tax this sum? As the result it turns out to be a Fine for Serving the Fatherland! This legalized action of people's deputies and ministers is the display of Wildness and Nonsense!

Besides, small business provides workplaces for other citizens without any efforts from officials. Therefore **family businesses, small businesses are providing minimum and necessary expenses on the activity and life, and they shouldn't be taxed.** On the contrary, small and family business has to be positively encouraged by government bodies by method of granting preferential terms of work and realization of work's product.

Medium business allows family to have higher level of comfort: to buy a car, to expand and improve housing, to go to the resort, to travel. The small contribution to the state fund in the form of a symbolical tax shouldn't liquidate advantage of medium business before small, because medium business makes bigger quantity of goods for people and considerably needs acquisition of the latest equipment.

Large business of a family has to pay a profit tax in a size that is established by the people and fills up a pension fund of workers.

Over large business of a family has s to fill a pension fund of the mini-state and voluntary to give the certain part of profit to the state's fund, exceeding profit of large business in a size that is established by the people. As a rule, over normal profit is useless for the owner's family. Therefore it is useful to direct its powerful part on cardinal improvement of living conditions of all the state's citizens and to innovative transformations of all types humanists and industrial production, instead of satisfaction their own unnatural, extreme, momentary requirements and entertainments.

Correction of the tax size (diminution) under accurate popular control is expedient to realize at an initiative, businessmen's voluntary investment of money to basic scientific researches, health care, education, the help to poor people, repair of roads, etc. Negative practice of life testifies: ignorant, immoral oligarchs can direct the profits on building of entertaining objects: casino, stadiums worth 3÷5 billion dollars, etc., instead of elimination negative, primitive living conditions of citizens (a problem with supply of clear water, lack of gas for housing heating, continuous interruptions in electricity, lack of housing for young families, etc.). Such disgrace shouldn't be in the reasonable, philanthropic state!

Sequence of transfer to reasonable and just way of life

The Mankind has reasonable, human examples of behaviour in the person of Sacred! Here all people would follow the example of them! Because the Kind attitude towards the helpless and left on concatenation of circumstances people, the voluntary possible help to all needing it, is the manifestation of high moral qualities of the Person! And it is useful to develop Activity of the people's Independence: "We will make everything quickly and well, we will not wait for the help from officials for life improvement! ".

The modern mankind exists similarly to fauna life: The ELEPHANT GOES, And SMALL DOGGIES BARK, rush to the Elephant, try to bite, demand from it to stop, to change the route. However, the BIG ELEPHANT continues SILENTLY to go its own WAY. Likewise the improvement of people's living conditions on the mother Earth will surely go in a reasonable way contrary to Wildness, Megalomania, Debauchery, the Perversion of the natural highly moral relations. Because the modern Mankind gradually approaches in consequence of contacts development, communication on television, tourism, training in institute of higher education, etc.

Modern people of all countries are guided by living conditions of the civilized countries of Europe and America. For example, men's dress code (jacket, trousers, shirt, tie, wrist watch, footwear, etc.) is already widespread in all countries. The women's clothes are gradually used in one style thanks to beauty contests and tourism. The violin, viola, a piano, wind and other perfect classical musical instruments gain the world distribution thanks to the international competitions of music. The generally accepted action is considered the creation of International Concerns and the Organizations. And an inexpensive production of essentials in insufficiently developed countries with the subsequent their delivery and sale in civilized countries promotes knowledge about new style of fashionable clothes and modern subjects of household appliances.

In such a way **THE GRADUAL OBJECTIVE RAPPROCHEMENT OF ALL THE PEOPLE** HAS ALREADY BEGUN TO ORIGINATE BY NATURAL WAY IN OUR TIME.

Now the analogue can be recollected: the standard philanthropic living conditions are 'Elephant', and nationalists are the 'Doggies' conducting with loud bark terrorist attacks, wars, radical violence. Poor judgment, self-admiration, gigantomania of small doggies would gradually degenerate as loudly they do not bark at the Civilized Elephant! The quicker people will understand and realize this simple Truth, this objective direction in development of humanity, the quicker will disappear poverty, hunger, unemployment, etc.

The process of gradual formation of the uniform state is useful to accompany with significant assistance to poor states from rich civilized countries. It will help people quicker to emerge from poverty and to reduce their mortality. Life of all people becomes more interesting, more productive and more reasonable. The human health and time of their life will increase. The advantage of this phenomenon is obvious!

The analysis of a current status of the international cooperation at the beginning of the XXI century AD allows to state manifestation of a global tendency of the reasonable organization of all people's life on Earth. In view of this objective circumstance **all people have to understand INEVITABILITY of formation the ONE, UNIFORM COUNTRY "EARTH"** with providing all people with minimum and necessary subsistence.

People

Once again we will understand the concept "**PEOPLE**" at the beginning of the subsequent reflections. In primitive tribes "people" was consisted of children, women and physically weak people, and also of active men with normal abilities. All adults elected the leader from among the strongest, bright and active members of a tribe. The leader acted only in interests of a tribe. All people from this tribe quietly, friendly and willingly carried out a decision of common meeting adult members of a tribe. Thus, during existence of tribes the concept "people" extended on **all** members of a tribe.

In the primitive states "mass" of simple people were chosen, and then approved the Governor thanks to his attractive personal qualities. There were re-elections of the state's leader at appearance of new, stronger personality. The concept "people" began to extend only on "masses", producers of material benefits. Since then the concept "People" became essential to differ from the concept "Governor".

So how to interpret the concept "People"? Thousand of nations? Or millions of working people? The answer is obvious. Then why to please units?

In the modern countries Governors, Presidents and others began to call themselves as «Servant of the People».

The False Servants of the People, as a rule, possess high level of admiration of the person, megalomania, permissiveness. They don't wish to look steadily at vital needs of simple people.

The Real Servants of the People have to possess ability accurately to see reality of citizens' life, to analyze possible options of the state progress, to offer on the confirmation to the PEOPLE (instead of to oligarchs) optimum actions of citizens. The full-fledged REASONABLE MANAGER CAN NOT AFFORD TO LIVE IN NATIONAL COUNTRY BETTER THAN COMMON WORKERING CITIZENS.

The real national uniform state has to be built on the base of Mind, Justice, Goodwill and Usefulness to the Simple Person to provide Life Progress on the Mother Earth.

Caring for Person

Let us consider the main, defining conditions of a natural people's hostel.

Primary, an initial action of the Citizen is to take care and create normal conditions of the birth, parenting and education of the child. Indispenzable observance of this law is to guarantee the reasonable prospect of all Mankind's development.

For implementation of the First Life Law is necessary to create in time the full-fledged conditions for formation of a family (housing, work, ETC).

It is useful for all to realize simple Truth: **"Pregnant Women are Invaluable Treasure on the Earth!"**. Therefore medical supervision, maternity hospital, food, tranquillity of soul and material security from the state have to be at an appropriate level!

Old People are also defenceless and physically weak. The helpless old age inevitably comes to each person at different times lives. In the modern world after a retirement many people become depreciate, superfluous and unneeded. Pensioners are disappointed on the last stage of life.

We are so mature workers, short-sighted!

Unlike children old men possess the invaluable capital: experience of emergence and solution of life's problems. And **Experience is that was proved it can't be disproved. Experience is Treasure!** It is the powerful, useful capital of people's life! It is possible not to repeat errors of last years by using the experiment of old people's life. Therefore it is expedient in each mini-state and on the whole Earth to form uniform community of old men - pensioners "**LIFE EXPERIENCE**" (or "**GENERAL COUNCIL OF VETERANS**" or "**WISDOM of VETERANS**").

Its voluntary functions are:

- information of all citizens about Useful and Harmful by means of television, printing editions, conferences, ETC;

- voluntary to visit lonely citizens with difficulties in possibility of movement and to help them to express the opinion during vote for adoption of laws;
- to carry out polite really feasible orders (requests) of Servants of the People, that is, Operating Executive Bodies of Democracy.

Advantage of the old wise person's aura consists in significant influence on mentality of the young and mature interlocutor. Therefore the pensioner, instead of vain, objectless, boring pro-driving ("murder") of time in the yard of block of flats, at the TV, gets opportunity to show activity of nature with awareness his usefulness to all citizens. Life at a stage of its end becomes fuller. In its turn, in response to useful activity of the pensioners, all workers will involuntarily increase the extent of their attention to daily needs and with pleasure give necessary help.

Modest Talents and Geniuses belong to the third category of weak defenceless people with unique abilities.

Foundation Stage of the Uniform Country "EARTH"

Dear citizens of the Earth, you shouldn't be afraid of changes habitual life for the **sake of Bright Future of Our Beloved Descendants!** Certainly, on re-education of people's psychology is necessary a lot of time (at least about three generations of lifetime).

It is necessary to make the accurate, detailed program of logical actions for effective movement to future the uniform country EARTH.

It is originally necessary to execute the main defining condition: to find individual wise persons and to give the floor to them in mass media. Then they will be able unassumingly,

144

gradually to designate modern wildness and nonsense of people's behaviour and to offer for understanding the reasonable ways of transformation life on the Earth. It also will be the beginning of bright Future in the next century.

On the first stage of transformation the people's living conditions on the planet it is necessary to carry out VOLUNTARY LEGAL DISBANDMENT of ALL EXISTING STATES.

Each people 's community with an identical way of life, with identical belief in correctness of their views on rules of behaviour, acquires the right for the organization of **the Mini-Republic** on the concrete ground with conditional border and to live in security, quietly, without violence just as you wish.

Not so big territory, smaller number of citizens allow more available, transparent, rationally, effectively to organize honest management of desirable living conditions.

If more deeply to think over the present, you will be able to find existence of a real tendency to a wise way of life and fair state activity. Certainly, it is wisely in advance to think over, estimate usefulness of all parts the Beautiful Plant of Novelty, before adoption of the final useful decision. And now in words, it seems to be, that everything is reasonable, useful, but the deeper reflection finds thoughtlessness and invisible the Root of All Evil as a result of statesmen's poor judgment.

In the first year of each mini-state's life ALL citizens will find their delusions, defects, estimate their size and plan an order of their elimination. In this process it is necessary carefully to consider the important circumstance: at the unreasonable, unfair organization of the power mini-state with short-sighted conditions of management and existence.

But life will accurately show to citizens the level and measure of justice function of such republic. And as in the small state a role and possibilities of simple citizens are significantly expanded, they will be able practically all quickly to gather and decide the destiny of unsuccessfully chosen Governors. Then new reasonable Managing directors will be elected with a task of obligatory observance by them of Goodwill and Usefulness to each citizen. Eventually, the useful, pleasant way of life will win and in these mini-states with unsuccessful primary form of a new type of management.

In the next years each mini-state's activities will have the process of improvement new conditions of its functioning. During this period it is useful to consider other mini-states' experience (negative and positive). As a result more reasonable standard device of the independent mini-state will be accepted by all citizens. Then it is expedient to take the most part of time reflections on establishment of rational, useful contacts with other mini-states. Thus there is only one an initial position: full freedom of people's movement through conditional border.

Certainly, **on the way to the Future appearance of conflicts** is inevitable between territorial communities of people. In such situations it is created the former power management of mini-state. Using nationalist patriotism and pronounced charm, leaders of the community easily and simply get possession of high authority govern the poorly educated obedient citizens. Thus the megalomania, self-confidence, desire to become god can lead to revival of attacks on the neighbouring mini-states. How and what to do the international body of management by process of living conditions transformation on the Earth? Certainly, it is possible quickly to destroy assailants. But under command of the wild nationalist simple innocent citizens are at war.

Therefore it is expedient to organize only blocking and full isolation the assailants' territory. All rapists can be told: "Live as you want, but don't harm an innocent people of the neighbouring mini-states".

A consequence of territory isolation surely will be sobering of simple citizens' mind, falling of their living standards and growing of discontent by actions of the impudent Governor. Such process can't last long. It will inevitably appear a manifestation of the high universal moral principles of life with desire to come back to a bosom of free contacts with all people in the world. Therefore you should not panic and to be very upset at emergence of such forcibly isolated mini-states with narrow minded governor, because such situation is temporary.

Reasonable and high-moral ways to the Future will inevitably navigate all conflicts. Why is there such confidence? Again we should remember the simple truth: Brain and Goodwill are very attractive to the Person's nature, because their domination creates Soul comfort!

In the next years movements to the Future will go the process of improvement all circumstances of citizens' life. Certainly, refusal from habitual form of the life, traditional concepts are very difficult, especially for elderly people, because their narrow thinking with habitual conditions should be eliminated for decades. The process of transformation their consciousness WITHOUT violence can be accomplished by belief and people encouragement. It will take at least a lifespan of three generations! During this period it is necessary to observe a quiet, imperceptible, natural type of transition the new human forms of functioning mini-state. Thus general reconciliation will automatically come between all people, and new reasonably well-mannered young generation will natural observe all established useful and adopted rules of life.

The Earth is immense for us, but the Earth is a small asterisk on the scale of the Space. Therefore we should not afraid the future transformation of mankind to one close-knit family, which is living on reasonable, benevolent laws with ONE LANGUAGE of COMMUNICATION of people on the all mother Earth. Primitive division of Mankind on a language sign has already FINISHED their existence. Languages of nationalities inevitably remain for philologists in the History.

In the present there is a real **dangerous situation:** Chinese gradually master all territories of the Earth. In the XXI century inhabitants of China became more than a half number of people on the Earth. For some unknown reason hardworking Chinese still have primitive grammar with using the conventional symbols in the form of **hieroglyphs!** Except China, hieroglyphs and conditional symbols are used in Korea, Japan, ETC. And this imperfection still exists, in spite of existence in civilized countries the rational, reasonable written fixation of Person's thoughts by means of rather small quantity of letters.

The knowledge of international language will significantly be facilitated by television broadcast the information transfers from the leading countries of the world when performing a condition of observance of a slow, correct, unambiguous equivalent of one sound to one letter and received pronunciation. It will allow each person independently to fulfil the pronunciation and literate sentences construction in different situations.

Coordination of the Uniform Country "EARTH"

It is expedient to carry out formation of Executive bodies of public authority from among reasonable citizens with pronounced natural qualities: Goodwill and Politeness.

The citizen with really high level of education in the Intelligent family will be able to organize and head the effective execution of reasonable ethic norms of citizens' life. To solve this problem effectively, at first it is necessary to create the rational conditions of adult citizens' vital activity. The vicious circle turns out: it is necessary to bring up new generation competently on the basis of high ethics, but people with bad education and with poor moral qualities won't be able to carry out it! How to be?

It is really only gradually to re-educate all citizens. Each new generation has to be grown up at successively high level of moral values. At the first stage of citizens' re-education they should be forced to follow the hostel's moral standards. Then this negative need will gradually disappear. It will give place to fixing in the person's nature of natural desire to live with the kind attitude towards people and to do something good not only for own cheek, but also for all people around.

Simple citizens have to begin and improve the selection run of the Authorized Performers of the People's Interests for creation future fair life. It is so simple! Because people with high level of ethics are much more than wild power-loving one. Therefore all people have to pay fixedly attention to worthy persons, to inform all citizens of the state about them and to delegate them powers of the useful Managing director. **Modern negative practice of a choice of the Managing director on party identification has to be essentially excluded!** Instead of parties it is possible to allow the organization only Communities of Fans of the nature, animals, birds, different types of art, tourism, sports, ETC.

In the people's country only those who works have to solve all local problems, "lives" daily, feels as nature, nerves, body and soul, all pluses and minuses of concrete life's situations. For example, in modern reality **the head of transport** goes by the excellent automobile car in the city. He **doesn't know the real conditions** of simple people's movement in the subway and buses. Therefore such "head" essentially can't competently be guided in arising problems of public transport. What is necessary? Yes, it is very simple: **the Executive Director of People Will (" the Servants of the People") has to "live" directly in the concrete field of activity, that is charged to him for the management,** i.å to move only in public transport (during the operational time)!

The history confirms existence of the Folk Wisdom, which saying in the form of accurate, short, clear, reasonable sayings and proverbs nobody could and won't be able to challenge. Therefore, **Folk Wisdom has the moral right** to develop laws of Mankind's life. IT is capable to provide Justice of creation and use of wise laws in interests of simple working people. Acceleration of a civilization's progress of all primary people communities will be provided on the way to creation the uniform country "EARTH".

In the people's country **Democratia = Demos (people) + Kratos (power) has to reign.**

In really democratic country (not according to the name, but actually) million simple Working Citizens have to develop wise rules of civilized communication in everyday life, and to control them in reality the **Democracies Authorized of Executive Body (DAEB) appointed by them have to.**

Free manifestation of the people's will is the main element of the competent, fair, effective, useful management of all spheres of citizens' life. For this purpose it is necessary to develop the rational, simple, available system of opinion fixation of each adult on each arisen problem of vital life.

It is known that all citizens quietly go to the work every day, therefore it isn't so difficult for them, for example, **every week** (or in two weeks), **in convenient time after work to express the personal opinion according to the solution of a**

150

question of any degree of importance. Convenient place for opinion fixation – in every quarter of the city and in each village.

Simple, available individual vote needs to be fixed by video camera with connection to electronic satellite system of tracking. Fixation process of the fact vote of the specific personality can be carried out with small expense of time (3 ÷ 4 minutes), for example:

- I showed in front of the camera one standard form with the image of the opened passport and an identification code against the current time, date and number of the concrete room,

- I came into the isolated cabin, read the text of the vote's subject and pressed the necessary button opposite "Yes" or "No" on an electronic plateau.

That's all, You are free!

In case of need voter can type the text of personal opinion on an electronic plateau.

The identification code and the photo of each citizen are registered in the unified state register (Registrum). Therefore, automatic comparison of the code and photo against surrounding concrete arrangement of vote's place with the code and photo in the register allows easily and authentically to control the validity of fixation process of the citizen's opinion. It is possible to find a false fake of vote. Gradually all citizens will get used to weekly performance of a civic duty with convenient registration of the fact the expression of personal opinion in the concrete district of the city and settlement. For simplification and an exception the manifestation of "forgetfulness" it is enough previously to place in the casual clothes only one copy of the small-sized standard form (the passport + code).

It is possible to vote in any point of universal suffrage during travel or a business trip to other area of the mini-state.

The economical weekly system of identification the people's wise opinion of the mini-state **excludes need** of education and use of the expensive modern Supreme Soviet. It is enough to use the system like "the Council of Ministers" for management of all branches of industrial production and coordination of economic activity of the mini-state's enterprises.

For all citizens it will become easier, fairer, more reasonable and more pleasant to live at such rational control system of all parties of functioning mini-state! Supremacy of Reason, Goodwill, Justice and Peace of Mind will be provided!

Just Laws of the Man's Life

It is necessary right now to designate useful, effective, durable Laws of Human's life for reasonable Future of Mankind.

It is not necessary to refer private, concrete norms of people's life because various situations are and will be an uncountable quantity to the concept "Law".

As a whole, **the LAW** is the only **essentially designated** standard of behaviour, actions of citizens for fair providing full-fledged human's life.

As a result of discussions **millions** working citizens (instead of thousands specialists lawyers) **are capable fully to designate wisely,** accurately, briefly, specifically Rational Grains of THEIR (instead of oligarchs) lives in all directions and to formulate **Life Laws**. It is rational once again to check accurately formulated text of the developed Law by ALL simple working citizens, and then to APPROVE it by means of open voting on a referendum of the simplified system.

Executive function of specialists-lawyers is rational to designate only a **preliminary** statement of a problem of life situations for public discussion by all citizens of the mini-state. Then the procedure of general specification of a final formulation of the text solution follows. Only after that it is possible to carry out procedure of universal suffrage of all adult citizens and the statement of the People's Opinion in the form of the Law Jurisprudentia.

In the false "people's" country the formation of life laws is getting through blinded experts on the basis of using the cunning concept "Truthful Lie" with a condition of observance oligarchs` benefit. As a result laws are filled with visible justice. However, in real life at their use there could be harm to people because of a small corner of authors` poor judgment during formation of laws.

It is necessary careful to select the identity of the judge at reasonable practice of the organization of the legal proceedings Jurisdiction (Lat.). Really, to be fair from the perspective of common sense the judge can work the person with faultless qualities of the Person's nature: honesty, decency, politeness, literacy in Jurisprudentia (Lat.) ETC. Only such personality can earn implicit confidence from citizens.

As it was considered in section 1.4, the modern system of protection of the accused possesses surprising property: it is capable effectively to protect practically ANY CRIMINAL! And lawyers as untouchable persons? How is it possible to justify and protect actions of the murderer and to despise the innocent victim? Where is your Conscience? The practical situation turns out: the modern law fasters Wildness in the person's nature and legalizes his ANTIHUMANITY!

Protection of the Criminal should not be in the future uniform country "Earth"! High moral education of citizens practically will exclude manifestation of false victim's testimonies. Accused has to explain his actions by himself in a court session.

In all known past times Reasonable Governors of the States aspired to deal with the mutual relations of citizens. Therefore they charged to clever persons to formulate rules of citizens' community: "The civil rights", "The relations between Oligarchs and simple Citizens", "The earth right and crop distribution", "War introduction ", "Rules of slaves activity ", etc.

Gradually after the XVIII century (Hammurabi) and the VIII century (Lycurgus) B.C. originated the development standards on the right of citizens "Jurisprudentia" in their practical use. For realization of these norms legal structures were created with the right to carry out proceedings "Jurisdictio". Process of development of Jurisprudentia and Jurisdictio generally was finished B.C. chronologies of human history.

In forming the Uniform Country the EARTH it is expedient to keep useful experience of Jurisprudentia and Jurisdictio with the new contents, which guaranteeing execution of the reasonable human basis. At their improvement it is enough to accept a simple initial position on the basis of the guaranteed observance of the main human values: Rationality and Goodwill for simple working citizens' good (not oligarchs).

Observance of the Justice

In the present it is rational to keep system of buildings widespread with small audiences for all interested persons for legal proceedings of Jurisdictio. In the modern world the useful experience is accumulated with the use of combination of the specialist–judge's knowledge and sober opinion of group simple citizens–jurors in the course of proceedings

("Jury trial"!). It should be kept during creation the country of Earth. The identity of the judge from among endowed by Nature citizens with special juridical education has to be chosen by general voting of all citizens this area of court's action (service). Only full confidence to honesty, goodwill, wisdom of the judge and jurors will provide the moral right to admit a judgment of Jurors definitive. It is useful to carry out execution of accepted judgment right after it was read by the judge.

Functions of peace officers increasingly will consist in "**reminder**"(instead of "power suppression") need of execution the beautiful, benevolent relations of people. In the modern states citizens practically don't see peace officers (police). The robber can act in a quiet situation. Residents and tourists have only visible impression: "everything is good, everything is normal, there is no any disorderly behaviour in the city!" However, to whom the attack victim will be able to address? In former times in the developed camps all city broke into districts with duty policemen in an attractive specific form. The distance between policemen was defined by visibility of the colleague. At any time citizens could see the guard and ask him for the help in a case of criminal attack or just for the inquiry. The attendant of the Order has to be the desirable, responsive GENTLEMAN for all citizens and tourists! Like so, the Attendant of the Order has to look and work in the Uniform Country "Earth"!

Employees of authorities, Representatives, Ministers, the President are Servants of the people. Therefore all officials have to get up "attention" before simple, without position at the power the working citizen and together think, consult, look for an exit from an impasse to satisfy a request within real opportunities.

The light-minded person-formalist by nature has no moral plan to hold a position 'the Authorized Performer', because at desire he will always find the reason for refusal to the visitor of body of public authority.

The useful Authorized Performer can be the person, possessing balanced level of a mental health, without manifestation of outburst of emotions, possessing controllability of the polite behaviour at contact with the visitor with any measure of good breeding and nature.

The responsible Authorized Performer of the people's will is elected by ALL inhabitants of the village, city, mini-state territory. The idlers, the indifferent people, despising the principles of reasonable life, not wishing to vote, according to the decision of all sane citizens can be deprived of nationality. You don't want to be the Citizen with obligatory execution of the citizen's functions – you won't be the Citizen legally. Like so – full freedom of acts without violence!

Presently in some civilized states terms specified of preliminary accommodation of people from other countries are established (from 5 to 15 years). The competitor gains the right to process 'Nationality' with all legal rights only after a faultless, harmless way of life. Seeing such respect for Nationality of the state, locals involuntarily, naturally reflect on need orderly to take part in the solution of any tasks, problems and life laws in the state without laziness and indifference manifestation. These circumstances naturally, without violence bring up citizens and descendants in the reasonable direction.

General Organization of Coordination (GOC)

At the second stage of transformations conditions of life on the Earth after understanding and elimination of negative situations in the world, it is possible to start the procedure of voluntary legal association in **the General Organization of Management** of all people's life on the planet Earth.

Its main functions are:

- fixation of information on each mini-state and the analysis of the arisen situations,
- formulation of recommendations and the offer them for using without violence,
- control and coordination of execution of useful recommendations,
- exchange of positive and negative life experience of the mini-states' citizens.

Gradually new main structures of actions coordination will be formed in GOC in process of the origination of demands. Mistakes in actions of heads-coordinators will be less and less.

Coordination of all main actions of the mini-states will gradually lead to depreciation of the concept "Country", turning it in symbolical, historical.

In consequence of reasonable alignment of living standards on the Earth will be inevitably begin the natural, peace, fair commonwealth of all people. **Almighty will be naturally satisfied with life of reasonable beings on a planet Earth!**

The word "Power" contains the concept "Force", "Violence" is more truly. Yes, it is necessary at the first stage of formation the uniform statehood. However, need for its use will gradually disappear according to progress of increase of mankind's moral portrait, its ability to have an open mind with the minimum poor judgment in concrete circumstances, satisfactions all new pleasant living conditions. At a stage of formation of the uniform country "EARTH" it is necessary to pass gradually from "Protection" of order of citizens` life to "Maintenance", "Providing", "Observance" of the normal, reasonable, rational, useful, effective and human relations of people.

By means of the computer equipment, the Internet, it is possible easily, simply to collect all information on opinion of citizens on the scale of the city, village, republic, all territorial communities for the analysis in GOC. As a result **the WILL of the PEOPLE of the UNIFORM COUNTRY** will be determined by the useful solution of a concrete life problem. It is **SUBJECT to OBLIGATORY EXECUTION!**

Television is the most effective general news media and discussion of problems, coordination of rational actions, education of high ethics, representation of Talented persons, etc.

The world television allows by the time of the beginning creation of the uniform country the EARTH significantly to expand possibilities of **general direct communication** of interlocutors. For this purpose it is necessary to provide settlements with stationary technical tools. This stationary equipment will also allow to provide accurate weekly universal suffrage of workers of the world without violations of the moral principles. This technology will provide to the central executive body of the state PEOPLE OF EARTH the full objective information in 24 hours of vote on the scale of the whole world. The programs developed by qualified professionals will be able automatically, without delay to provide results of weekly votes to the people and executive bodies of GOC.

It is useful to have the following main programs of the Central Television of the Uniform Country PEOPLE OF EARTH: 'What Does the Person Need to Know, 'How to Help the Nature', 'Perfection of a Soul and a Body', 'Health',

'The Reasonable Solution of Problems', 'Let's Think', 'Our Abilities', 'A Kind Wish', 'Refined Manners', 'Mind and Reason', 'Comfort of a Soul and a Body', 'Dictatorship of the Reason of the People', 'Facts of Life', 'Our Talents', 'Geniuses of the Mankind', 'Precious Time of Life', 'Kinds of the Person's Nature', 'The Language of General Communication', 'The Useful Education', 'A Plate of Nonsense', 'The Truth Tree', 'The Truth Kingdom', 'The Natural Beginning of the Person', 'Grace, Honour and Conscience', 'Life Is Beautiful', 'Science Highlights', 'Intellect and Intelligence', 'Our Opportunities', 'We Are Such ...', 'The Reasonable Future', 'A Way to Comfort a Soul and a Body', etc.

The author hopes for reasonable reader's perception of the program of creation the uniform country the EARTH, made by the simple intellectually working person at the request of Almighty God.

The bitter truth shouldn't cause You, dear reader, to feel excessive negative emotions. Thank You for the shown interest for need of creation the reasonable, fair, full-fledged, pleasant Future of the Mankind. All of us are inhabitants of ONE planet.

CHOOGIN Valeriy Vitalievich

2015 AD.

www.ingramcontent.com/pod-product-compliance
Lightning Source LLC
Chambersburg PA
CBHW020019030726
47499CB00007B/2188